Letter to Sarah and Other Stories

AMY KRISTOFF

Deer Run Press
Cushing, Maine

Copyright © 2024 Amy Kristoff.

All rights reserved. No part this book may be reproduced or transmitted in any form or by any means, electronic or mechanical, including photo-copying, recording, or by any information storage and retrieval system, without written permission from the copyright owner.

This is a work of fiction. Names, characters, places and incidents either are the product of the author's imagination or are used fictitiously, and any resemblance to any actual persons (living or dead), events, or locales is entirely coincidental.

Library of Congress Card Number: 2024940420

ISBN: 978-1-937869-24-3

First Printing, 2024

Published by
Deer Run Press
8 Cushing Road
Cushing, ME 04563

Contents

Letter to Sarah//1

The Lucky Girl //42

No One Winner //61

Party Time—Not!//72

Mother Knows Best//81

Letter to Sarah

Dear Sarah,

I'm writing this because I need perspective. I wasn't allowed any by my family. I forgave them all, however, if only because not one of them treated me poorly (but some were definitely nicer than others), even if not all of them liked me.

Where to begin? I will start with the summer I was eleven, the first time I was sent from hot Phoenix, Arizona to Georgetown, Kentucky, the summer of 1977. I had never before left Arizona and went on an airplane for the first time, to meet my aunt Candace and uncle Martin. I wasn't worried about leaving my supposedly grieving mother, Corrine, behind, as she didn't appear to be too upset. When your husband walked to the corner bar seven nights a week for a few years and didn't return home one morning because he'd wandered into the street and was killed by a hit-and-run driver, it figured something like that finally happened.

One thing I didn't have much of was clothes. My mother worked part-time at a drycleaners and brought home any mending that needed to be done, so she seemed to think that qualified her as a seamstress. She claimed that since I would be growing "until who knew when," there was no reason to let me wear anything other than what she'd sewed, which didn't amount to much. The second Aunt Candace saw me at Blue Grass Airport in Lexington, she could hardly wait to say, "We need to take you shopping," after having greeted me. In turn I became self-conscious about how I appeared to the rest of the world. Then she threw me off by adding, "But it's nice to see you again." (I'd had an escort when I had deplaned, so Aunt Candace had to know it was me.)

I didn't bother correcting her regarding saying "again" by mistake. How could I when I was in awe of her? She was much prettier than my dowdy mother, who seemed to be hell-bent on making me dowdy, too. Besides, adults were always right, what I was raised to believe.

Aunt Candace drove me to her and Uncle Martin's "Forever Farm," in her silver Jaguar sedan. Just seeing the countryside fly by the window was worth having come all this way. Even though it was a rather humid June day, it was wonderful compared to Phoenix and the unrelenting sun and heat. I hadn't even arrived at the farm, and I was already dreading leaving at summer's end. However, I'd been tentatively promised this trip every summer until I graduated from high school. I didn't dare ask what happened after that because it seemed so far in the future.

I probably would have tried to resist returning to Arizona after that first summer, except I had the distinct impression Uncle Martin really didn't enjoy having me around. I wanted to think I was imagining as much, but I was certain I was right.

Forever Farm was so big it was impossible to see the house from Paddock Drive, the main road. I had been living with my parents in a cramped, two-bedroom bungalow, and the exterior was wanting for space as well, given how close the neighbors' houses were on either side of ours as well as behind it. Therefore, the farm wasn't quite as huge as it seemed at the time, but 250 acres does cover quite a lot of ground. After driving a third of a mile (but it appeared longer), Aunt Candace made a sharp right turn and went uphill to reach a large, white Georgian Colonial with a generous parking area in front. We might as well have come upon a replica of the White House, I was so impressed. I got out

Letter to Sarah

of the car and downhill from the house could see two large, white brick horse barns with black trim on the Dutch doors, sitting side-by-side, connected by a breezeway. White plank fencing extended as far as the tree line, several hundred yards in the distance. Although I was too young for romantic love, I had fallen in love with this place.

Noticing me gravitating toward the barns, Aunt Candace said, "Come inside, I'll introduce you to Uncle Martin and show you where you'll be sleeping. I say it like that because you'll probably be spending most of your time outside, if I'm guessing correctly."

As soon as I entered the house, there was an aroma of apple-cinnamon, and Aunt Candace mentioned she'd just baked an apple pie before picking me up at the airport. I wasn't sure if I was supposed to thank her, as in she'd baked it to celebrate my arrival? Maybe I was the only one who was super-excited. Then she said, "Follow me to Uncle Martin's office. It's downstairs, across from the kitchen. Your room is right next door. The rest of the bedrooms are upstairs, but down here you'll have a bathroom connected to your room, rather than having to cross a hallway. If you'd rather be upstairs at some point, I can get a room ready. And down here you don't have to remove your shoes unless you're going to be in here awhile. I'm not a stickler about cleanliness, but no barn shoes in any bedrooms, please."

I was standing behind Aunt Candace by this time, and she was about to knock on the closed office door of Uncle Martin's. Before she did, however, she whispered, "Uncle Martin has turned the office into a bedroom, but he has his own bathroom so you won't have to share. He's wanted it this way ever since his accident almost twelve years ago." Then after knocking on the door and being given the O.K. to enter, Aunt Candace did so, with me right behind. In the oak-paneled room sat stone-faced Uncle Martin, in a wheelchair. Whatever had happened to him had never been revealed to me. Had I been too young? Surely my mother knew about the situation.

Rudely (I thought) looking me up and down a couple times, Uncle Martin muttered, "She's gonna be taller than you. It would have been nice if Corrine could have deigned to send some pictures every once in awhile."

Immediately I thought about my mother having declared I was doomed to grow "until who knew when." Evidently she was correct. At least I made an effort to shake hands, although Uncle Martin wasn't interested in being polite.

Aunt Candace remarked, "Corrine used to send some here and there but hadn't lately and I didn't want to bother her about it. I never would have guessed you cared."

In response, Uncle Martin spun his wheelchair around, not saying another word. I didn't know what to think. He still owned his trucking business at this point and we'd technically interrupted him at work, so maybe he was having a bad day.

I just wanted to go to the barn! First, however, I was instructed to retrieve my suitcase from the car and unpack. Afterward Aunt Candace would accompany me. I dreaded the possibility she would insist upon accompanying me to the barn every time, which would make it a very long summer.

Fortunately my worry was unfounded, as Aunt Candace declared, "Once you get your footing around here, I'll be able to let you do more and more on your own. I may even put you in charge of feeding the horses a couple mornings and evenings a week. That'll give my help, Max Sheridan, some free time, which he doesn't get a whole lot of. He's my only full-time employee. You'll be meeting him as soon as he returns from the feed store."

Was the guy going to be around a lot? I wanted to pretend the place was mine and I lived here alone, so I hoped not.

Aunt Candace had met me at the airport with her long blonde hair hanging loose, but she had put it in a ponytail, slipped through the back of a white painter's cap, to go to the barn. She still had on the jeans and red T-shirt she'd worn earlier but changed from her blue leather sandals to a pair of black leather paddock boots. She looked like she could have been modeling for an ad in a horse magazine, although she was already fifty. She probably never had kids because she didn't want to lose her figure, I assumed.

The paved driveway passed the house and continued to the barns, and there was also a path of crushed stone that ran parallel to the driveway, beginning at the side of the house. Aunt Candace explained Uncle Martin had created the path to jog on, and it was a mile from one end to the other and back. It had been worth every penny because it spared his knees from the hard pounding on pavement. Under her breath she added, "So much for it being an issue anymore."

Entering the first barn, it was difficult to see anything at first because it was rather dark, although the back door was wide open. Halfway down the aisleway made a "T", leading to the breezeway on the left, a service door on the right. The other barn was actually a riding arena, which made sense, given its size. Several of the windows were closed because there was hay stored in the empty stalls. There was a steel-tube gate across the opened back doorway, and the broodmares were in an area just inside the barn, milling around eating hay while their babies napped. I had never been face-to-face with a horse and here were several of them. If there hadn't been a second gate to prevent the horses from having the run of the whole barn, I would have walked right up to them. I knew nothing about horses but neither did I have any fear of them.

I stood next to Aunt Candace while she mentioned the stable name of each broodmare: the gray was "Lollie"; the chestnut with the white spot on her forehead was "Dot"; the other chestnut was "Betsy"; and the bay was "Marcy." None of the foals yet had stable (versus registered) names, so I was welcome to decide what they should be.

There was a rumble out front and Aunt Candace said, "Sounds like Max is back." Then she went to see him while I remained by the horses. Perhaps I was being rude, but I was in no hurry to meet "the help."

I continued to watch the mares eating hay, and Lollie's foal sat up. She sniffed his side for a few seconds before returning to munching hay. I hoped the foal would try to stand, but he proceeded to lay back down on his side. I watched everyone for a couple more minutes and then turned around, wondering what happened to Aunt Candace. I couldn't see her, so I was about to walk back to the front of the barn when she reappeared, Mr. Sheridan beside her. I turned back around to watch the horses, waiting to be introduced to him.

Still observing the horses, I had a name for Lollie's foal, whose coat was much darker than his dam's, almost black: "King" (as in "King Coal"). Then I thought "Prince" would be more fitting, given his age. Aunt Candace then tapped my shoulder, saying, "Sadie, I would like to introduce you to Max Sheridan."

"Pleased to meet you, Sadie," Max said, as we shook hands. "Tall, dark, and handsome" aptly described him, and his reception was the opposite of Uncle Martin's, which was greatly appreciated. If Uncle Martin felt threatened by Max, it wouldn't have been surprising. The only thing he was probably missing was having plenty of money. Aunt Candace (and her sister) didn't come from a family that had a lot, so it was important to both of them, although it appeared my mother hadn't exactly hit the jackpot. Nonetheless, it was a safe bet she was in love with her husband until his untimely death. How else could it have been explained, she'd stay with someone who was addicted to alcohol like he was? Meanwhile, whatever spark Aunt Candace might have had with Uncle Martin seemed to be long gone.

"You ride, Sadie?" Max wanted to know. He was standing very close and looking at me intently.

"I'm going to teach her," Aunt Candace interjected. I was glad she did because I was embarrassed to admit I'd never

Letter to Sarah

before ridden a horse, let alone the fact this was the first time I'd seen one.

"You'll be in good hands," Max said, "provided your aunt picks the right horse. She and your uncle breed them and she shows a little, so no one horse is a 'lesson horse.'"

"I think Lollie would be O.K. for lessons once her foal is weaned."

"How about Domino?"

"He's kind of big for her, but he is definitely laid-back."

"Sadie, Domino was a racehorse bred here and now he's a show horse. How cool is that?"

I nodded, trying to take all this in, and Aunt Candace remarked, "What isn't cool is how the trailer is still sitting in the arena from last winter because I didn't bother to show this year."

"There's still time."

Aunt Candace shook her head and turned away. Who appeared then but her two yellow Labrador retrievers, "Daisy" and "Mandy": "Hello ladies! I was just wondering where you were." Then she leaned over to pet them. Her life would have been empty without them, and their dual tail-wagging was welcomed.

***

Martin never was easy to love, but the fact he was very wealthy had certainly helped. And he'd had to build his wealth back up following a lengthy divorce from his first wife, Adrienne. He absolutely was not getting divorced again. Candace knew not to file for divorce, and as much as she wanted to love him "forever," she couldn't. She tried to content herself with the fact she'd waited until she was thirty-five to marry, and her husband was a decade her senior. Longevity did not run in his family, as both his parents passed away in their late fifties.

Initially Candace was ashamed of her "marital restlessness." At the same time she was proud of the fact her husband trusted her enough to add her name to the deed for the horse farm he'd purchased after his divorce was final and he was in a spending mood. The first three years of their marriage, Candace managed the farm and took care of the horses, with occasional help from Martin. Out of the blue he hired a good friend's son to be a caretaker/ handyman/groom. Initially Candace considered the man's presence an intrusion and hadn't appreciated not being consulted about the matter. Plainly Martin was trying to do his friend (and his friend's son Max) a favor. However, it wasn't long before the guy became indispensable, as he was very helpful around the farm and was a capable horseman. Since Candace spent so much time with him, she ended up seducing him and felt justified! The affair seemed so harmless, especially since Max was single and Martin was always at work, running his thriving trucking business. The brief time he'd been single while owning the farm, he'd hired part-time help from neighboring horse properties. Sometimes it seemed as if he'd purchased the farm just to brag about it. He was minimally experienced working with horses and could barely ride but was obsessed with racing bloodlines and was determined to breed the next Kentucky Derby winner. None of the horses he'd bred had amounted to much, and Candace had had more success with a few of them in the show hunter and jumper rings once their racing careers were over. She'd even sold a couple for quite a lot of money, which appeared to impress Martin.

Candace had her mother, Catherine, to thank for the innate riding ability she possessed. The latter was raised on a northern Arizona cattle ranch, "Two Pines," and was on a horse with her mother, Marcia, before she could even walk. Marcia helped her husband, Randy, with the cattle, as he was short-handed quite often. Having a new baby didn't deter her in the least. The forty-acre ranch was adjacent to hundreds of acres of grazing land leased from the Bureau of Land Management. Catherine became engaged to the only

Letter to Sarah

boy she ever dated in high school, Andrew Rye. After graduation he headed to college and veterinary school in Colorado while Catherine made good on her promise to wait for him, staying on at her parents' ranch, helping however she could. She barely saw her fiancé until he completed his studies and had his license to practice veterinary medicine in his home state of Arizona.

Following a simple wedding ceremony in front of family and close friends, Catherine and Andrew ended up moving in with her parents. The plan was to eventually build another house on the property. Andrew worked for "Northern Arizona Veterinary Services" and his truck was basically his office, as there were long drives between calls. With student loans to pay off, having financial independence seemed to be in the distant future.

Then Catherine's father became ill, and she was needed more than ever at the ranch. It wasn't long before his illness took a toll on Marcia, as she was his caretaker. The decision was made by them to quit the cattle business and relocate to Phoenix, where Randy had been seeing a specialist. Whatever profit they could eke out of the sale of their ranch, as well as the equipment, horses and cattle, would go toward purchasing a modest house, the remainder put in retirement savings.

Catherine and Andrew ended up following her parents to Phoenix, where Andrew's salary was almost double, working at an equine clinic. Also, he wouldn't have to put so many miles on his truck.

Living in a studio apartment, the couple saved for a house. Catherine was hired as an assistant trainer at "S and S Quarter Horses," a showing and training stable in Scottsdale. It wasn't long before the couple was able to purchase a two-acre horse property that not only happened to be in a horse-friendly subdivision but was within easy walking distance to S and S Quarter Horses. Feeling like they had some roots, they decided to start a family, and the grandparents enjoyed spending time with their grandchildren. Andrew's parents, Lena and Kurt, still lived "up north" and were in good health. Catherine's weren't faring quite as well, but the change of climate, scenery and lifestyle benefited them overall.

***

I still needed to unpack my suitcase, but I was in no hurry to go in the house. Just as Aunt Candace had predicted, I wanted to be outside as much as possible. I couldn't wait to have her teach me some basics about horses, and soon I could help take care of them. My mother always had a list of things for me to do around the house, so I was accustomed to at least some responsibility. Above all, I wanted to impress Aunt Candace.

Upon Aunt Candace's and my return to the house, I noticed Daisy and Mandy had followed us. Max had remained in the barn, as he still had some stalls to clean. Uncle Martin was on the back porch, in his wheelchair. His expression had softened, and he even appeared slightly curious about me. It couldn't have been emphasized enough, I wanted to not only fit in with the household but be able to contribute any way I could, including helping Uncle Martin with whatever he needed done.

Uncle Martin asked, "How'd she do? Going to be a horse person, too?"

"If I had to bet money, I'd put it on 'yes,'" Aunt Candace replied.

"Should have left her at the barn. Make her work until feeding time."

"Don't be ridiculous, Martin. I was just going to throw something together for our 'feeding time' and then we'll head back down there. She'll be a fast learner, I can tell."

***

Letter to Sarah

Several months after Candace had initiated her love affair with Max Sheridan, she suddenly decided it was time to end it. In fact, she'd spent the night before in bed with her husband, which wasn't unusual, but she'd intended to confess the whole thing to him. Then she'd thought better of it after failing (yet again) to elicit any affection from him. It had been so long since they'd been intimate, even an embrace was too much to expect. Her next plan was to tell Max once he arrived to help feed the horses breakfast, it was over. Even if her husband never again made love to her, at least she would no longer be deceiving him. As it was, if the affair initially seemed harmless, it no longer was because she was in love with Max and was positive he felt the same way about her.

Candace heard Max's truck outside the barn as she was finishing feeding hay to the horses, having already given all of them their grain. Max greeted her and then remarked, "You must have gotten an awful early start to be almost done feeding. You trying to take my job away?"

"We need to talk, Max," Candace said.

"Uh-oh. You just said my name, and the only time you say it is when we are . . ."

"I got it."

"I can see by your expression you're not 'in the mood,' for sure."

After pushing the hay cart out of the way, Candace stood close to Max and declared, "We have to end things. Now. Forever."

Clearly shocked, Max stepped back and said, "You're just messing with me, aren't you?"

Shaking her head, Candace had to bite her lip to keep from crying. Finally she was able to mumble, "No."

Max looked upward for a couple seconds and then looked at Candace. He too shook his head. Then he turned around as if to leave.

Candace grabbed the metal handle of the hay cart and pushed the cart back to the stall it had been stored in, a couple dozen feet away. Afterward she turned around and found herself in Max's arms, and he murmured he loved her. Candace couldn't help telling him she loved him too, and they passionately kissed.

Suddenly Martin appeared and bellowed, "Busted! And I didn't even have to catch you two shits in bed! I give my friend's son a good job and a decent paycheck, and he screws my wife! I should have known when I married her, she'd do something like this to me!" Then he spun around and went back in the direction he came, toward the house.

Max said, "I'm toast now, but I don't care. I deserve it."

"No you don't," Candace told him. "I started it. Let me go talk to him."

Martin had ridden to the barn in an electric golf cart, which he used more often than not, "to save time." About halfway to the house the battery died. Uttering a stream of curses, he got out and rapidly walked the rest of the way, disappearing into the house. Candace walked much slower, collecting her thoughts. She knew he wouldn't divorce her, but she needed to remind him he was the one who'd hired Max, essentially "asking for it." In other words, there was plenty of blame to go around, Martin's "issues" aside. Hopefully that would give him some perspective.

Candace entered the house via the front door, as it was unlocked. After removing her paddock shoes she went upstairs, figuring it was where Martin had gone. If he had taken his shoes off, they wouldn't be by the door. However, he was probably so upset he left them on, yet he was extremely meticulous.

At the top of the stairs was the first time Candace really looked up, and she about fell backward because Martin was standing right there. He was a pretty big man, and his anger made him appear even larger. Never before had he physically harmed Candace, but she was suddenly fearful he might hit her. She deserved it more than Max deserved to lose his job.

This was hardly the time to be concerned with whether or

Letter to Sarah

not Martin was still wearing his shoes, but Candace couldn't resist looking down to see. It would help her gauge how furious he was. A slight shift of her head turned out to be a lucky move because Martin took a swing at her at the same moment, and she confirmed he'd removed his shoes and was only wearing socks. He not only missed her head, the force behind the punch was so great he spun around like he was ice skating, lost his balance and fell backward down the hardwood stairs. It seemed like it happened in slow motion, yet there was nothing Candace could have done to help. Had he left his shoes on, the accident might have been prevented.

***

After lunch I unpacked my things, and it didn't take long because I hadn't brought much. Aunt Candace was expected to take me shopping a few times and buy me clothes, saving my mother from having to do any more sewing. Even if my mother had a lot of money she would have scrimped and saved every penny she could. Aunt Candace too knew the value of a dollar but was more willing to splurge.

As I was about to exit "my" bedroom, some movement outside the window caught my eye. Max was out there, having apparently come from the barn. He waved, and I thought he was waving at me, so I waved too. Then Aunt Candace appeared, as she was most likely on the deck, and went down the four-step, side stairway. She hurried up to Max and whispered something in his ear, the sight of which blew me away, particularly because he wasn't her husband. Then she turned to leave but not before Max swatted her butt – and she smiled! Whatever those two had going, I decided Uncle Martin hadn't a clue. He was supposedly taking a post-lunch nap, but how could Aunt Candace be so certain? I wasn't sure I should be looking forward to the summer here because Uncle Martin might blow his stack if he saw those two flirt-

Amy Kristoff

ing. To describe him as humorless was an understatement. If he had been friendly (not to mention awake at this point in time) I would have immediately told him what I saw. There was no predicting how he would have reacted.

***

Candace believed in adhering to her marriage vows regarding the part about "in sickness and in health," following Martin's accident. As it was, he still had no intention of divorcing, despite having been humiliated by her cheating. When he finally felt better, he apologized for having mistreated her. Candace told him she was sorry too, and it appeared their marriage would improve if only because of Martin's new-found respect for her.

There was good news for Martin regarding his prognosis: he would regain 100% mobility, provided he was disciplined about his recovery efforts. Candace had been happy for him, but he appeared indignant to have been told he'd be good as new again. That was the first indication he was going to move forward with anger and resentment.

Naturally one of Martin's main concerns was keeping his business going, and fortunately he had a couple longtime employees who were able to step up and take on more responsibilities. Meanwhile, Candace would continue to take care of the farm and the horses, and Max would be staying on to help with the same. Firing him was never mentioned by Martin, even in passing. As it was, Candace would need Max more than ever because a lot of her time would be taken up caring for Martin until he got on his feet again. Although he hadn't broken his back, he'd torn some ligaments and fractured a couple ribs as well as some toes on his left foot. He decided the best way to get around was in a wheelchair, and he became attached to it. Luckily the house had wide doorways.

Martin convalesced at home for a couple weeks, following

Letter to Sarah

a brief hospital stay, and he proceeded to become even more attached to the wheelchair. It wasn't long before it was difficult for him to get up on his own and walk. He appeared pleased with himself.

Naturally Candace thought Martin was punishing her as much as himself by letting himself potentially become incapacitated. As it was, their love life was over, so it was just as well they no longer shared a bed. He could have ascended the stairs to their bedroom eventually, but he was making sure it was impossible to recover enough to do so.

Even though Martin could have continued use the golf cart to get around the farm, he completely lost interest in ever visiting the horses, not to mention enjoying the outdoors. He couldn't have cared less about his jogging path. All this should have meant Candace and Max could have resumed their affair, but they carried on like they'd each taken a vow of abstinence as well as silence.

One morning Candace awoke feeling really blah. It was an especially lousy day to have this problem because Max was in Florida with his mother, visiting his sick aunt. He would in fact be gone all week because they'd driven down there, so Candace was in charge of all the barn work. Fortunately the foals were already weaned and were temporarily in the back pasture day and night, so there were less stalls to clean. However, they still needed to be watered and fed grain.

By the time Candace finished her chores she felt even worse, and it finally occurred to her she might be pregnant. She and Max never used protection because they hadn't fooled around that much, which was admittedly a lame excuse. She hadn't otherwise been concerned about birth control because her husband was impotent.

As soon as Candace had a chance she drove into Georgetown and picked up a pregnancy test at the drugstore. Fearful though she was of the result, she went back home and took the test. It was positive. A trip to her doctor late the next day confirmed as much. When Candace and her husband (in absentia) were congratulated by Dr. Gail Olmar, Candace just nodded. She could only imagine what Martin intended to do for an encore once he got the news.

***

Finally Aunt Candace gave the go-ahead to return to the barn for the afternoon. Daisy and Mandy still needed their lunch, so I would be shown where their food was stored and how much they were allotted. After that I was going to help Aunt Candace clean the area where the mares and their foals had been eating hay and napping. She mentioned maybe riding Domino if there was enough time before she had to get back to the house. I assumed that meant she had to help Uncle Martin in some way. I still couldn't tell if he wasn't able to walk or simply refused to. Either way it made sense he was crabby because who could live like that? I felt sorry for Aunt Candace, but she appeared to take her husband's behavior in stride.

Aunt Candace let the horses outside before we started cleaning the pen. I watched Lollie's foal, and "Prince" still seemed like a good name for him. Dot's solid chestnut foal's coat was the color of a fall leaf, so I thought "Autumn" would be appropriate. The other chestnut mare was Betsy, whose foal wasn't nearly as striking as Dot's, and he was smaller. I thought "Junior" was a fitting name. The bay mare, Marcy, had a filly, who was the same color as her mother and very delicate-looking. I couldn't think of a name for her off-hand, so I'd think about it.

Having been handed a pitchfork, I started cleaning the pen, following how Aunt Candace was doing so with her pitchfork—placing any soiled hay and sawdust in a black cart that was larger than the one she used for the hay. In no time at all, however, the cart was full. She took it back through the gate and down the aisle, disappearing out the

Letter to Sarah

front doorway. I didn't know where she dumped all the barn refuse, so it was possible she'd be gone awhile. I stood in the opened back doorway and watched the horses in the pasture. All the mares were grazing, and the colts were playing but couldn't quite get excited. It was pretty humid by this time of the day, so maybe that was the reason. The filly appeared to be the least interested in socializing and didn't want to stick by her mother, so she was grazing by herself. I turned around and there was Uncle Martin, in his wheelchair, on the far side of the pen, watching me. I still couldn't fathom why he detested me, and I felt I at least deserved a chance before he made his decision.

I kept hoping Aunt Candace would return with the cart, and in the meantime it seemed like Uncle Martin and I were going to have a stare-down. I hated to turn my back on him and return to watching the horses, but I really didn't have a choice.

Finally Uncle Martin broke the silence, remarking "All those babies were born in March and they already look old enough to wean, except for maybe the one chestnut mare's."

I nodded. There was more awkward silence, so I started sifting through the extra hay and bedding, pretending I was working. Then Uncle Martin added, "You know, you have a lot in common with those young horses."

That remark completely threw me off, and I had no idea what to say. Fortunately Aunt Candace returned and we finished cleaning the pen. The second time the cart had to be dumped, I went with her. Uncle Martin stuck around until then, continuing to watch me. Aunt Candace either accepted his behavior or didn't notice, so I was forced to do both. Maybe she was happy her husband finally came to the barn, at the expense of him making me feel self-conscious.

Max returned from wherever he went and parked his truck in front of the barn. He probably didn't initially know Uncle Martin was in here, but Uncle Martin soon emerged from the shadows and told Aunt Candace he'd see her at the house. She nodded at her husband but didn't appear to be paying any attention to him because she was looking at Max. They looked like two people in love, yet I honestly had never before witnessed it first-hand. My mother might have loved my father, but it wasn't reciprocated.

Once it appeared the coast was clear (Uncle Martin had left), Max pulled a small, green velvet box with a purple ribbon out of his shirt pocket and handed it to me. Aunt Candace looked amazed but very pleased. I must have appeared hesitant to accept the gift because Max said, "Go ahead and open it, Sadie. Happy Birthday, by the way. It's the fifteenth, is it not? I couldn't wait that long."

The present was a beautiful, 14k gold I.D. bracelet with "Sadie" on it, a tiny horseshoe etched next to my name. There was also a gold horse charm attached to one of the links.

It felt awkward thanking someone I didn't know for such a generous gift, but I nonetheless did so. Max said I was welcome in return. Even though Aunt Candace initially appeared surprised by the gesture, she might have been behind the effort. There was definitely something going on between those two. Aunt Candace was a different person with Max, versus with her husband.

***

One thing Martin never lacked was an appetite, so Candace decided to satisfy his craving for a favorite dish of his and afterward tell him she was expecting. The simplicity of her plan was reassuring, although she would do no assuming, regarding his reaction to the news. She needed to decide what to prepare that would put him in the best possible mood.

At dinner time Candace didn't feel like eating, which wasn't surprising, given how nervous she was. She'd even prepared something she too enjoyed: lamb riblets, having made a special trip to the supermarket for all the ingredients. Her

Letter to Sarah

lack of desire to eat incited Martin to ask what the hell her problem was, since he knew she liked this dish. Candace proceeded to excuse herself from the table and went in the bathroom to throw up.

***

    Dinner tonight was fried chicken. Aunt Candace had prepared the batter and put the chicken pieces in the oven before going in Uncle Martin's room to help him bathe—or so she said. This was the first real lull in the day, and since the horses had been fed their evening meal, Aunt Candace probably wouldn't be going back down there until the next day. Even the dogs were finally settled in the house. I intended to wait until after dinner to take a shower, so I kept my new bracelet on, wanting to wear it at the table. Naturally I had no idea what the possible implication might be for doing so.
    Anyway, dinner time had arrived none too soon because I was starving, despite having eaten plenty for lunch. I plopped down in one of the ladder-backed dining room chairs, across from Uncle Martin, who was once again sitting in his wheelchair. The table was large and oblong-shaped, so it seemed like there was plenty of room between us, at least at first. Aunt Candace had told me to have a seat, rather than help her, so it wasn't like I hadn't attempted to be of some use. I wanted to tell Uncle Martin as much so he'd quit scowling at me. However, I was starting to realize I'd have to get used to it.
    Aunt Candace had poured Uncle Martin a glass of wine, and in no time at all he'd finished it. Rather than hold off on drinking another glass, he wanted another one immediately and called to her in the kitchen, to bring the whole bottle. Then the phone could be heard ringing, so she said she'd be there in a minute. The potato salad was already on the table, and I almost served myself some.
    Meanwhile, Uncle Martin asked me, "Remember what I

said earlier today about you having a lot in common with those young horses?"

"Yes."

"What I was trying to infer is you too started your life here, girl."

I nodded, not comprehending what he was getting at. However, there was obviously something to what he'd just said because he'd sat back in his wheelchair and nodded too, looking smug.

Soon afterward, Aunt Candace reappeared with the wine bottle. She must have heard what Uncle Martin said because she looked tempted to hit him over the head with it! After pouring him a glass of wine, she started to leave again with the bottle.

"Leave the bottle right here," Uncle Martin said, hitting the left side of the table with his (left) hand.

"Martin, you don't need—"

"I am not going to argue, Candace."

"I'm not either," she said and placed the wine bottle where Uncle Martin wanted it before going back in the kitchen. Soon afterward she returned with a large plate piled high with delicious-looking fried chicken. There was enough for way more than the three of us. Uncle Martin was a big man, so maybe he would eat a lot of it. At lunch he'd barely eaten anything because he was more interested in scowling at me.

It appeared Uncle Martin was finally content to eat, and Aunt Candace had served him three pieces of chicken and a large spoonful of potato salad. She then placed two pieces of chicken and a nearly equally generous serving of potato salad on my plate. I started eating the chicken first, using my fingers. It was still very warm, so I decided to eat some of the potato salad and then return to the chicken.

I used a fork to dig into the potato salad, my new bracelet on my left wrist, the same hand I used to hold utensils. Uncle Martin looked up from eating a drumstick and dropped it on his plate upon noticing the bracelet. It was still light outside, and the candlestick bulbs in the fixture above the table appeared to make the bracelet gleam. He wanted to know, "What's that on your wrist, girl?"

"Her name's Sadie, Martin," Aunt Candace said, looking ready to kill him.

"I can call her whatever the hell I want," Uncle Martin remarked while staring at me.

"Her name's Sadie," Aunt Candace repeated.

"I know. . . What's on your wrist, Sadie?"

"A bracelet."

"It's beautiful. Who gave it to you?"

"I did," Aunt Candace said before I could even begin to say Max's name. "Her birthday is coming up soon."

I nodded and kept my mouth shut, other than to put food in it (and I went back to eating a piece of chicken). Evidently Max wasn't supposed to have given me the bracelet. I felt like I'd done something I should have been ashamed of, but I couldn't fathom what it was. Neither Aunt Candace nor Uncle Martin appeared inclined to enlighten me.

***

My mother called Aunt Candace after dinner, and they talked for a couple minutes. We were in the den, and I was a few feet away, watching TV. Aunt Candace must have been asked if I was available, as she put her hand over the phone receiver and asked me if I wanted to talk to my mother. I'd never before been offered a choice regarding something I felt obligated to do, and in this case I shook my head! Aunt Candace nodded in return and told my mother, "She must have stepped outside with the dogs. If you want to wait a minute, I . . . You're sure? . . . O.K. . . . Next time I'll call you and I'll make certain she's close by."

As much as I loved my mother, I felt more at home here with Aunt Candace. That was especially notable when taking into account how Uncle Martin never failed to display his dislike of me. It came in handy he mostly kept to himself, so far anyway. Aunt Candace had mentioned Uncle Martin would have been miserable if he didn't have his business, but he seemed pretty miserable nonetheless. Maybe she'd meant he would have been even more miserable if his trucking business didn't make the money it did. The upkeep of the farm had to be expensive, and that wasn't including the care and feeding of the horses as well as Max's salary.

***

I should have fallen asleep the second my head hit the pillow, but that wasn't the case. Perhaps I should have skipped eating a piece of the apple pie Aunt Candace had baked, as I felt very full. At home I was never offered so much food. Aunt Candace was a better cook than my mother, but I didn't tell her that. Then again in a way I did because I told her the dinner was the best meal I'd ever eaten. My mother was never interested in putting time into making anything tasty. The two sisters couldn't have been more different in their youth and that never changed. Supposedly my mother never liked to be around horses, while Aunt Candace was as obsessed with them as their mother, Catherine. My mother didn't even care for the outdoors.

Grandma Rye passed away shortly before I was born, so I never got to meet her. Having lost the love of her life, Andrew, after a long battle with cancer, she essentially died of a broken heart.

As soon as I finally started to feel drowsy, a banging sound could be heard, coming from Uncle Martin's room. It sounded like he was literally hitting his head against the wall! I wanted to find that funny but couldn't. Even though he'd thus far been anything but friendly, I felt kind of sorry for him.

Rather than count sheep, I tried to think of a name for

Letter to Sarah

the filly of Marcy's. Something starting with an "M," like her name: Mindy? Mandy? The latter wouldn't work because Aunt Candace already had Mandy the dog. I thought of "Misty" and liked the sound of that name.

Then Aunt Candace could be heard talking quite loudly to Uncle Martin, but what she said was indistinguishable. It didn't sound like Uncle Martin said a word. Meanwhile, Aunt Candace continued talking but her voice became more quiet. At least she put a stop to the banging. Maybe it bothered Uncle Martin, I was in the next room? The last thing I wanted was to get on his nerves and then be sent right back to Arizona. That sounded so depressing I closed my eyes and soon fell asleep.

***

When I awoke the next morning, birds could be heard chirping. The drape for the one window in my room was open, so there was plenty of light coming in. I hadn't set an alarm and was disappointed Aunt Candace hadn't made sure I was up. I pushed the covers away and sat up. After stretching my arms over my head for a couple seconds, my feet were on the floor and I was changing from my pajamas to a pair of jeans and a T-shirt. My bracelet was on the dresser, and I decided to leave it there for the day. I didn't want to catch it on something while I was in the barn.

There didn't appear to be anyone in the house, until I heard Uncle Martin's voice. He must have been on the phone. Other than that the only sound was the pendulum on a wall clock, at the end of the hallway. I stuck my head in the kitchen entryway, and it appeared breakfast was long over. Aunt Candace must have gone to the barn, so that was where I went.

A white pickup truck with "Marcus Veterinary Clinic" painted in blue on the sides was parked in front of the stall barn, Max's older, red pickup next to it. Lollie and her foal,

Prince, were in the first stall on the right. Dr. Marcus was in there, attending to the latter while Aunt Candace stood outside the stall, watching. "Good morning," she said upon seeing me.

"Hello," I answered. "What happened?"

"Lollie's baby got hurt. We still haven't figured out how. Max is walking around the pasture behind the barn right now, trying to find the cause. It figures, something happens to my favorite, not that I don't like them all. I was just cleaning up after breakfast when Max came and told me the colt was bloody from a puncture wound. I was just going to check on you again and see if you were up. I'd checked on you earlier and you looked peaceful so I thought I'd let you sleep."

I wanted to be of some use, so I asked, "Is it O.K. if I help Max?"

"Only until Doc Marcus leaves," Aunt Candace replied. "Then we're going to the house so I can make you some breakfast."

I wasn't that hungry and would have preferred to stay and help Max. Compared to at home, I felt like all I did was eat. Admittedly I was more active here, but still. Besides, my mother already complained about me growing until who knew when (and Uncle Martin had his own remark), so I didn't need to encourage my body with exercise and nourishment! However, that didn't appear to be a consideration of Aunt Candace's.

***

Candace was noticeably pregnant before Martin finally couldn't resist making rude comments, usually under his breath, which made them all the more hurtful. She could never figure out why those bothered her the most. Meanwhile, if Max was aware of her condition, he did an excellent job of pretending not to notice. By the eighth month she finally couldn't take it anymore and had to confront him. She felt ready to burst in more ways than one.

The three-car garage was perpendicular to the front of the house, and the garden tractor was stored in there. It was used to mow around the house and the barns. Max was in the driveway, changing the mower blades. It was a beautiful May afternoon, the temperature around 70 degrees. As Candace approached him, he appeared oblivious to her presence, how he'd been ever since she'd told them they had to end things (other than their brief exchange that triggered Martin's meltdown). If he'd had any idea she was pregnant, he would have known the baby was his.

"Hi," Candace said. He had just finished putting on the new blades but was still kneeling. Either he was into staring at the tractor and the black-topped driveway or he was continuing to avoid her. She really couldn't take it anymore!

"Hey," Max finally said in return but wouldn't even look up, let alone stand.

"Could you please look at me for two seconds?"

"Huh?" he answered but did stand, albeit reluctantly. Still, he wouldn't make eye contact with her.

"How can I say this?" Candace began, suddenly self-conscious. "I need you to really look at me because what's going on concerns you too, damn it!"

Finally, after eight months (but it seemed like eight years to Candace) Max did look at her, and his eyes went to the bump under the loose-fitting, short-sleeved, brown cotton blouse she was wearing untucked and suddenly he "got it." Although he appeared ready to faint, he quickly recovered and hugged her, being overly careful. She hugged him back with far less tentativeness and wanted to tell him, "The baby won't break if you hold me a little!" It seemed like a miracle he was even daring to get near her, and she wasn't worried about Martin seeing them together. Instead, she enjoyed the moment and didn't feel so alone, if temporarily. She wanted nothing more than to have Max's emotional support.

Amy Kristoff

Candace's sister, Corrine, was aware of the situation and had been a willing listener. Since Corrine lived in Arizona, their communication was limited to letters and the occasional phone call. Corrine had offered more than once, to help her sister any way she could. Little did she know, her older sister was considering taking her up on that offer, but it would be a huge favor on Corrine's part. Candace had yet to tell her husband what she had in mind to do, but she was almost certain he would go along with it. "All" he had to do was compensate his sister-in-law financially. It would be a lot cheaper than splitting everything down the middle in a divorce settlement.

***

Somehow I deserved blueberry pancakes for breakfast. I was determined I wasn't hungry until taking a bite of them and proceeded to eat the whole stack. Aunt Candace was evidently accustomed to serving Uncle Martin, who had a big appetite. She went to the supermarket a lot, while Max did most of the errand-running for the farm and anything horse-related. Uncle Martin spent the whole day on the phone. Even though I had yet to see him not in the wheelchair, he had to be capable of walking, if only short distances. Otherwise, given all he ate, he'd weigh even more than he did.

My favorite activity thus far was hanging around the barn, just like the dogs, happy to be there. Then Aunt Candace invited me to help her brush and tack up Domino for a ride. Feeling overstuffed with pancakes, I was eager to go back to the barn and do something. Domino was in a pasture right behind the arena, turned out with another gelding who had just finished his racing career and was convalescing.

With the indoor riding arena's main doors open, it was comfortable in there, so Aunt Candace put Domino through

Letter to Sarah

his paces inside and then told me it was my turn, after putting a longe line over his bridle. She just wanted me to get a feel for sitting on a horse and I could borrow her helmet "next time." She never wore one at home, so it wasn't readily available. Before I knew it I was practically thrown on Domino's back. However, I wasn't scared and to the contrary was excited, as I completely trusted Aunt Candace's judgement. He slowly walked in a circle while she gave me pointers on how to properly sit in an English saddle. I was having the time of my life, even though I didn't know what I was doing!

Max was in the barn when we returned, and I blabbed about having just "ridden" Domino, which was out of character. He congratulated me and appeared genuinely pleased. I couldn't get over how much friendlier he was than Uncle Martin. If nothing else, Max's attitude proved money didn't buy happiness.

It turned out to be quite a long day at the barn, as Aunt Candace decided all the mares and foals (besides Lollie and Prince) needed to be brought inside and put in separate stalls. It was time for the babies to start getting accustomed to this kind of living arrangement. She also wanted Max to help her handle all of them for a few minutes apiece. There were also two horses that needed to be brought in from a pasture east of the one Domino was in with his buddy. It didn't have any type of shelter, and the forecast was calling for heavy showers in the late afternoon or evening.

By three, most of the horse-related work was done, and Max was sticking around to feed, so Aunt Candace and I returned to the house, the dogs right behind. Since dinner wasn't too far away, she asked if I was hungry for a late lunch, or did I want to wait to eat? I told her I didn't mind waiting and was tired more than anything. Otherwise I would have asked to stay at the barn and help Max with the last feeding. I expected my stamina to build up and eventually I'd become accustomed to the humidity.

I left my shoes by the door and went straight to my room,

intending to put on my bracelet. I wanted to wear it while I watched some TV. Or maybe I should take a shower first? I didn't think I was going back to the barn, so maybe taking a shower was a good idea. Nonetheless, I wanted to look at my new bracelet beforehand.

It wasn't on the dresser. That was impossible unless someone stole it, and the only person who could have done so was Uncle Martin, which was ridiculous!

The question was whether or not to tell Aunt Candace. Or was it better to wait and pretend as if the bracelet hadn't disappeared? It was possible Uncle Martin wouldn't be able to help but ask me at dinner, why I wasn't wearing it. I wished a clever comeback would occur to me, should the occasion arise. Then again, I'd never have the nerve.

***

It seemed too good to be true for Corrine, her sister was finally going to have her rich husband send her some money. That was how Corrine thought of the situation that was presented to her. There was never enough money in the Wexler household, despite Corrine working at a drycleaners as well as doing all the mending for the company. Her forever-drunk husband, Samuel, never held a good-paying job long enough to "profit" from as much. Corrine was inherently thrifty and never felt like she was wanting for anything, but extra income was always welcomed. Still, she wanted to help her sister, first and foremost, despite initially claiming it was a money issue.

Corrine didn't even bother asking for "permission" from Samuel to take on a responsibility, since she would in turn be receiving a check every month. It was impossible he would have a problem with the arrangement because it would help take the pressure off him to hold a job. In other words, he'd have more time (and disposable income) to go out and get drunk. She was aware this attitude made her an enabler, but since she didn't drink, she had no idea how insidious her husband's addiction was.

Samuel and Corrine didn't have kids because of his drinking, which was to say he had "performance issues." Candace had once revealed her husband, Martin, too had "issues," but she wasn't specific. However, when Candace disclosed she was pregnant, Corrine wondered who the father was and marveled her sister "got away with having an affair." After all, Martin would never forgive Candace for cheating but wouldn't divorce her. Candace had put up with plenty of emotional abuse over the years, so maybe the affair was her way of rebelling. She always was headstrong.

Martin was allowing Candace to keep the baby for a year and it was Corrine's turn to step in. Candace wasn't exactly maternal, so that would be interesting. Admittedly, Corrine wasn't maternal either, and she would be "the real mother" from one year on.

***

I found out at dinner, Uncle Martin would be gone the following day, from early morning until late afternoon. A woman named "Becky" was picking him up. From the conversation between Aunt Candace and him, it sounded like she might be a secretary at his business. I didn't pay too much attention to the brief exchange because all I could think about was sneaking into his room while he was gone and looking for my bracelet. It had to be in there somewhere. Even if I found it, then what? If I took it, he'd know I was the one who'd been snooping around. Nonetheless, all I could think about was getting it back.

Uncle Martin didn't even look in my direction during dinner, let alone make a comment about my bracelet (or lack thereof). I actually missed having him scowl at me! I must have liked the attention. Meanwhile, he appeared preoccupied and kept his conversation with Aunt Candace to a minimum. Maybe they'd had an argument earlier. She didn't serve him wine with the meal, so was that a factor in his behavior? Back at home, there was always some form of alcohol at the dinner table, although my mother never touched any of it. Once my father imbibed whatever was available, off to the neighborhood bar he went. He was "lucky" there was a place within easy walking distance, until his fateful demise.

Beef stew was the main course, and Uncle Martin had foregone a utensil to eat it with and instead dipped chunks of Italian bread in his stew bowl. I couldn't help but furtively watch him, astounded by his gluttony! Given his size it obviously took quite a lot of food to fill him up, but it still seemed like he could have used some restraint. Meanwhile, Aunt Candace was picking at her portion, using a fork. Maybe she wasn't hungry. She sure didn't look happy.

***

Candace saw little of herself in her new baby, but she determined there were semblances galore of Max. As interested as he was in the newborn, maintaining his distance was necessary, to avoid potentially upsetting Martin. It was anyone's guess how angry Martin truly was, but he appeared to take the situation in stride. The bottom line was he had to accept the situation for financial reasons. Perhaps since he didn't have kids of his own, there was always a chance he would eventually embrace the fact his wife provided him with an heiress of sorts.

A year passed in no time at all, and the day came for Candace to say good-bye to her daughter, whose first name was "Sarah." Corrine happened to detest that name and wanted to change it. Candace wasn't about to argue and told her sister to do what was necessary to deal with her new lifestyle and responsibilities. Sarah would still be Sarah to Candace.

Letter to Sarah

***

Uncle Martin wasn't exactly subtle about his early morning departure and woke me up. The clock on the nightstand read 4:30! It was impossible he was unaware of how loud he was. This time around, however, it didn't sound like he was banging his head against the wall. Since I was awake I wanted to see him leave, to confirm he could walk on his own. When it sounded like he was making his departure I would open my door, but he couldn't know he was being spied on.

Once Uncle Martin finally finished making noise, he opened his door. I threw back the covers, leaped out of bed and ran to the door, slowly opening it. He had his back to me, a black leather duffel bag on his shoulder, and was walking, albeit slowly. I started to open my door a little more when he said, "Crap!" and turned back around to re-enter his room. I shut my door again in the meantime, and it appeared he hadn't noticed me. My heart felt like it was in my throat, thanks to the close call. Aunt Candace had to know her husband could walk on his own, so why did she appear to be in denial?

I went back to bed and slept soundly for three hours. Awaking with a start, I felt like I'd overslept again. The horses were typically fed by six-thirty or seven every morning, so I had probably missed out.

The house was quiet, so I figured Aunt Candace was at the barn with Daisy and Mandy. I went through the kitchen to depart, and it didn't look like Aunt Candace had made any breakfast. There wasn't even a pot of coffee brewing. Maybe she decided to skip eating since Uncle Martin was away.

Daisy and Mandy were sitting in the doorway of the stall barn, so Aunt Candace had to be around. Max's pickup was nowhere to be seen, so I assumed he wasn't here. Several of the horses neighed upon my entrance, which indicated Aunt Candace had not yet fed them. I wished I'd been given instructions to feed everyone, including the dogs.

Amy Kristoff

***

Although Candace vowed to be more careful about getting pregnant again, she had no intention of hiding her feelings for Max. Sarah had just been shipped off to Arizona, as Martin had one of his female employees fly there with the baby and hand her off to Corrine, right in the airport terminal, and then fly back to Kentucky. Candace was relieved not to have had the responsibility because she wouldn't have been able to part with her daughter under those circumstances.

Anyway, Candace's take on the matter of seducing Max again was, what did she have to lose? Her pregnancy had cemented Martin's disapproval of her, despite his new-found, if temporary, respect for her following his accident. As it was, he probably assumed she and Max had never ended their affair. There was no point in trying to explain that wasn't the case. Nonetheless, she still loved him.

Candace was pretty sure Max hadn't been seeing anyone during their "hiatus," which was very encouraging. Even if he had been, she wasn't deterred. He had saved her from her belligerent and eccentric husband. If Max was over her, she would accept as much (but hopefully she wouldn't have to).

Martin had taken a rare trip to his office in downtown Lexington, and Candace was certain he'd left (versus "pretending" he'd done so) because an employee had picked him up. Even though he used the wheelchair all the time in the house, he did walk from his room to the waiting truck. His black Lincoln was collecting dust in the garage because he was given a ride everywhere. She kept telling him if he didn't move around more using his own two feet, he would be using the wheelchair all the time, whether he wanted to or not. It was anyone's guess if there was a wheelchair awaiting him at the office.

Anyway, with Martin gone for at least part of the day, Candace traipsed down to the barn, in search of Max. With

Letter to Sarah

all the horses turned out and the stalls cleaned, he was in the tack room, putting leather conditioner on some bridles that were little-used. He briefly turned his head when she entered, and she stopped right behind him and put her arms around his waist. He continued applying conditioner to the bridle he'd been working on, so she moved her hands lower. He stopped what he was doing and turned around.

***

I walked back to the house to have breakfast. The dogs stayed put, which should have led me to conclude Aunt Candace was in the barn. Rather than wonder why she hadn't fed the horses, I was preoccupied. It wasn't until I neared the house did I see Max's truck parked in the driveway. It was most likely there when I'd left the house, but it would have been impossible to see unless I'd turned around after walking at least a hundred yards. I wasn't sure what was going on, but I thought I had an idea.

Opening the kitchen door, I found myself face-to-face with Max, who warmly greeted me but couldn't wait to depart for the barn.

Since there was nowhere besides the barn I wanted to be, I went back down there after breakfast. It was doubtful I'd walk in on Aunt Candace and Max sharing an intimate moment because they were so guarded about demonstrating their feelings for one another. With Uncle Martin temporarily away, they had evidently decided to spend some time together, however.

Max had already fed the horses in the barn, although Lollie and her foal Prince (the one who was injured) were turned out beforehand so he could clean their stall and then bring them back inside. Prince was supposed to remain confined as much as possible for a week and not play or run around.

When I went in the barn, Max was in fact cleaning Lollie

and Prince's stall. He said, "Sadie, I have something for you, I just found."

I went over to the stall and he handed over my bracelet! It was all grimy and the horse charm was missing. "Where did you find this?" I asked him.

"It was in here," he replied. "It must have fallen off your wrist, although the clasp doesn't appear to be broken."

I wanted to say, "That's because Uncle Martin threw it in there! Nothing broke, other than the charm having been yanked off the bracelet by him!" Instead I merely thanked him.

Then Aunt Candace appeared, from the direction of the house. Daisy and Mandy must have been at the barn the whole time because they'd wandered down here out of habit after they'd been let outside. "Good morning," she said and then wanted to know what was going on.

"I'd left the bracelet Max gave me on the dresser in my room but it disappeared. I didn't say anything because it would have seemed like I was accusing 'someone' of stealing it. It turned out it was in a stall."

"You mean Uncle Martin might have taken it?"

I nodded, compelling Aunt Candace to put her arm around me, doing so to console herself more so than me. I still couldn't figure out what I had done to deserve having Uncle Martin treat me like this.

Aunt Candace offered to clean the bracelet, so I gave it to her. Once I had it back, I would keep it out of plain sight and wouldn't wear it anymore until I got home. Even though I liked that plan, I didn't feel any better about the whole situation.

***

How Candace and Martin met was definitely coincidental, if only because they came from such different backgrounds. Candace had moved to Lexington at 25, having worked at

Letter to Sarah

racetracks in California and Arizona. She thought the vibe was too laid-back and wanted to see what another part of the racehorse world as well as the country had to offer, namely breeding farms in the Lexington area.

Relying on references in some cases and in others sheer nerve, Candace drove up numerous (and impressive if only because of their lengths) driveways of various Lexington area breeding farms. The latter was what got her an interview that led to being hired on the spot at fifty-acre "Double Dutch Farm." The married owner was not only short-handed but expected her to have an affair. Candace never wanted to be the cause of a marriage break-up unless it was her own! Her single-mindedness about horses had helped keep her on the straight and narrow (for the most part).

Ironically, Double Dutch Farm was where she first saw her future husband, as Martin happened to know her boss, Archer Beem, on a business and personal level. Mr. Beem's racehorses were a hobby, and Martin had dropped off some documents relative to his trucking business and Mr. Beem's packaging company. Candace had been in the barn brushing a horse that Mr. Beem was going to send to a sale. Mr. Beem was looking over the horse while she worked, and Martin looked Candace over. She was glad he soon left. He certainly didn't appear to give a whit about horses. A couple years later she moved to 100-acre "Stowaway Stables," about a mile away because the pay was a lot better. Also, she had more experience with horses than what her many farm tasks entailed at Double Dutch. She decided her boss gave her non-horse-related jobs to be vindictive, since she wasn't interested in him romantically.

By this time Martin was researching racehorse bloodlines and fantasizing about owning his own breeding farm. He was at Stowaway Stables to check out the ideal criteria of racehorse breeding stallions, of which they had two. Tall and overbearing-looking, there was an aura about him that Candace couldn't get out of her mind, despite initially finding him unsettling. This time around, however, he appeared to ignore her, which bothered her!

It was years later when Candace and Martin saw one another yet again. She had moved to "Blue Ribbon Thoroughbreds," just outside Georgetown. She lived on the seventy-five acre farm in a swanky, open-concept apartment (stainless steel appliances and wood floors) above the stalls, which were in a renovated dairy barn. The main house was an 8,000 square foot English Tudor with an in-ground pool and a tennis court in the backyard. Martin was actually there to look at the property, with the expectation the owners might be planning on listing it. A Realtor-friend had made the arrangement for him to make the visit, so he could potentially be the first one to make an offer.

Martin was not only a man of few words, he cut right to the point when he did speak. Seeing Candace again, he walked right up to her as she was raking the crushed gravel behind the barn. At first he just stared at her and she felt "lucky" for having been noticed by him again. However, she ignored him and kept raking, so he got her attention by removing the rake from her grip and proceeding to lean over and kiss her right hand! Afterward he said, "I had to do that since we keep running into one another. I propose we go out. Or I can simply propose. I finally finished divorcing my wife, and I'm looking for a farm. If I buy this place, you could stay on, even if you don't want to marry me."

Candace must have looked mortified because Martin managed to crack a smile for a couple seconds, proving he had a sense of humor (sort of). She remained slightly creeped out by Martin but couldn't stop thinking about him. At times she was ashamed of herself for finding any allure whatsoever in the guy. Although she was aware one of the attractions was his apparent wealth, she couldn't help herself!

A year later, Martin came calling again at Blue Ribbon—for Candace! The property still wasn't listed, so he'd have to settle for her and forget about the farm because the owners

Letter to Sarah

had decided to stay put indefinitely. As for Candace, how could she refuse a date with a man who decided he liked horses and wanted a farm of his own? (She didn't know at the time he'd since purchased a place.) She'd feel like a fool if she didn't "go for it." Money never failed to buy happiness, did it?

***

It must have already been discussed between Aunt Candace and Max, he needed to get the trailer ready for a show because he immediately pulled it out of the arena with his truck, after cleaning the stalls. I was helping Aunt Candace brush Domino, which was a project because he had managed to get very dirty. She said, "I'll get Domino worked down a little, and you can help Max set up a couple cross-rails for us to pop over." Although somewhat self-taught in regard to jumping, Aunt Candace had also received enough instruction over the years to know about gauging distances and finding a spot in front of each jump. That was especially helpful because she never even wore a helmet at home, not even to jump. She only wore one at the shows.

A potential problem was Domino hadn't been jumped in several months and didn't particularly miss it. Also, Aunt Candace appeared more intent on showing off than anything else. Whatever the case she wasn't paying any attention to Domino's demeanor as he was trotted toward the first cross-rail. Given his slow pace and Aunt Candace's vast amount of riding experience, it appeared impossible she'd fall off. However, she did, as Domino darted to the right of the fence at the last second. She sailed right over the fence, landing headfirst on the far side of it. Although the floor of the arena had plenty of sand, it didn't appear to do much to break her fall.

Max looked absolutely shocked, but he quickly sprang into action, attending to Aunt Candace. As he was leaning over her, he nodded in the direction of where Domino was standing, the reins still around his neck and said, "Sadie, if you could, please slowly approach Domino and grab hold of his reins. If he starts to run off, let him go."

Domino stood still, so Max told me to carefully pull the reins over the horse's head so I would have something more substantial to hold onto. Again, the horse quietly stood, which was a relief. I remained beside him while Max concentrated on trying to get Aunt Candace to regain consciousness. He was talking to her and holding her shoulders. She must have heard him because it appeared she nodded a couple times. Finally she held her head up, which was another huge relief. Max must have asked her if he ought to call for an ambulance because she replied, "I'm not going to the hospital! I'll be fine! I'm fine right now, just a little fuzzy-feeling. Just let me lie here for a couple minutes. Put Domino away and I'll see about getting up when you return."

"Sure you didn't break anything?"

"No! I'm fine! Just let me be for a minute or two."

Max left her and came over to lead Domino back to his stall. I followed them, expecting to be of some use untacking the horse, so Max could return to Aunt Candace sooner. She definitely wasn't herself, and Max's ashen face said it all.

Postscript

A fourteen-carat yellow gold bracelet with "Sarah" engraved on it was a present from an unlikely source: Uncle Martin, on my 21st birthday, shortly before he passed away. The one Aunt Candace never got around to cleaning, I finally did. However, I never wore it again because after all, my name was Sarah. I liked it a lot better than Sadie, and my "real aunt" (Corrine) accepted the fact I wanted to be called who I really was. It took years for Uncle Martin to accept me (as a family member). I was aware he was under no obligation. Following his wife's death, he continued to be resentful

Letter to Sarah

of me, but I stuck it out at the farm for the summer. Aunt Corrine didn't fly in for the funeral, as Uncle Martin wouldn't pay for her ticket. He and Aunt Candace (I still referred to her as my aunt, despite knowing the truth) hadn't attended Uncle Samuel's funeral in Arizona because Uncle Martin despised him. There was always an excuse in this family, to help explain its dysfunction. Maybe everyone's was like that.

The lady named Becky moved in even before Aunt Candace's wake and became the housekeeper. She had no interest in the horses, so she spent the whole day cleaning and cooking. Uncle Martin spent the entire day in his room/office, on the phone, just like before. However, he magically ditched the wheelchair.

Max worked more hours than ever, taking care of the farm and the horses. Uncle Martin probably didn't pay him for all the extra time. Max never outright told me he was my father because he seemed self-conscious about the whole situation. Also, he worried about my financial stability, so he let Uncle Martin get used to the notion he had an heir if he would so choose.

At the end of that first summer, Uncle Martin did in fact invite me to return the following year. He said "everyone" would still be there, so I took that to mean Max would be around. Becky admittedly did keep the house cleaner than Aunt Candace, but she complained all the time about Daisy and Mandy being allowed inside. She was pretty nice to me "despite knowing who I really was."

The drive to Aunt Candace's funeral was the one occasion Uncle Martin, Max, and I went somewhere together. Uncle Martin let Max drive his Lincoln, and we sat in the back. It was amazing, the number of people who showed up for the funeral. Uncle Martin claimed the wake the evening before was "even worse" as far as the number of attendees. There was only a large turnout at either one because of him, not Aunt Candace (so he said). He never introduced me as anyone other than "a family friend" (a nameless one at that). All

I could think was I lost my mother yet I had only spent a little over a year with her, and most of that time I was too young to appreciate as much! I must have been in shock because of everything that had happened in such short order, as I had yet to shed a tear.

Back home afterward, Uncle Martin invited Max to sit on the deck and share a bottle of brandy. It was cloudy but very warm. Max accepted the invitation, and both men removed their suit coats and ties and rolled up their shirt sleeves. They looked more like they were about to do some physical work, not sit and talk (and drink). The last thing I wanted was to be anywhere near them, so I went to the barn. Daisy and Mandy followed me, and Max called out, it was O.K. to feed them lunch since they hadn't yet eaten. I was glad to have a chore and wished I could work with the horses without still needing supervision. Nonetheless I would find something to do, even if it was sweeping the tack room floor. I had a feeling a loud argument was going to ensue.

Unfortunately there was nothing to provide a sound barrier between the back of the house and the barns. Also, the air was almost still, so no wind could drown out some of the possibly contentious exchange. I didn't hear anything for a few minutes, as they were probably busy downing their first round of drinks. Then Max exclaimed, "So what did you use to stab the gray colt when he was in the pasture?"

"Quit accusing me!" Uncle Martin replied. "I told you I had nothing to do with that. You and Candace never kept the barns and pastures up like they needed to be, so the colt got into something. If she hadn't been like a mare in heat, you both might have gotten some work done! Besides, I'd been in a wheelchair. I couldn't have gone out there if I wanted."

"Liar."

"Say that again?"

"Liar!"

"You always did have more nerve than you knew what to do with, Max, I gotta hand it to you. I can see how you and

Letter to Sarah

she clicked so well. It's no secret she married me for the money, but at least she didn't bother pretending otherwise. I loved her for that alone."

"Bullshit. You never loved her. You wouldn't have a clue."

Then there was silence, so I looked up at the house, expecting to see the two men still sitting there. Instead, one of the them was sprawled out on the deck. When Uncle Martin stood and slowly lumbered into the house, I knew Max was the one who was down for the count. Uncle Martin was either ashamed of what he did or was already too drunk to care. I finally sat down, my back against one of the stalls, and cried. Daisy and Mandy appeared and sat beside me, one on either side.

Aunt Candace was my mother and I loved her, along with Forever Farm.

Love,

Me

The Lucky Girl

Four years! That was how long since Bern had, well, you know. The divorce from his beloved wife, Michaela, hadn't been easy, as he obviously was still in love with her. They'd had one last fling right as the moving truck was being driven away with her half (for the most part) of the stuff they'd acquired in the five short years they'd been married (they'd lived together for two years prior). The fact Bern's livelihood came before her, never helped, especially since she loved plenty of attention. He since came to realize he was better off with a woman who was as horse crazy as he was. The problem was most women who were into horses were just plain crazy. That made them great for dating and fun in the sack, but that was it! He was getting older, and it was time to settle down. His dream woman would be young and naïve enough he could basically mold her into what he wanted in a wife: one who would work side-by-side with him in the barn all day and not get sick of it. Then, in the evening, they could talk shop and watch TV. It didn't sound like too much to ask for, but he had yet to meet/find the female who could meet the simple criteria. Admittedly, Bern hadn't exactly been going out of his way to find his dream girl, if only because he refused to appear desperate. He preferred to wait (forever, if necessary) rather than search the world over for her and come up empty-handed.

Then, about nine a.m. this morning, Bern received a text from his cousin, Julie, who lived about an hour due south in Delaplane, Indiana, and had a horse boarding stable. He was

Letter to Sarah

up here in Shady Cove, about thirty-five miles southeast of Chicago. She had a neighbor, Heather Turner, who had been helping with the barn chores for the past four years and wanted to ride for a trainer – English or Western, she rode both equally well. She had been homeschooled since moving to Delaplane from Mesa, Arizona at thirteen and was 17, already finished with high school (or its equivalent). She wanted to be a horse trainer and didn't want to bother with college, but her parents wanted her to take her time deciding. In the meantime, she would be allowed to work for a trainer for a couple months. She had competed extensively in the Southwest at Paint and Quarter Horse shows, riding horses for other people because her parents never bought her a horse of her own. However, they'd lived in a horse-friendly community in Mesa and where they currently resided was semi-rural.

Included with the text was a short video of Heather riding a tall, lanky bay, her seat perfect in the hunt saddle. She was a natural, no doubt about it. Then Bern zeroed in on her face (as best as he could see it), and he swore she looked like a noticeably younger version of his ex. Immediately he became obsessed with this girl. It was imperative she at least visit him and let him feast his eyes upon her. He became excited at the mere thought, but no one could even suspect he was thinking like this. It wasn't like he was a sexual predator. Overall he was a great guy! (Loneliness did this to even the best of individuals.)

Bern texted Julie: "Put in a good word for me! Summer's almost here and horses need to be ready for shows! Even if she can't jump I can teach her and she can flat some."

She texted back: "I already did! It's why you're getting a video! Anything 4 U!"

Bern texted a happy face emoji and five exclamation points in response. Hopefully it didn't reveal too much enthusiasm. He loved Julie like she was his sister, in part because neither one of them had any siblings and had spent a lot of time together, growing up. Their respective families used to extensively show on the hunter-jumper circuit in the Midwest, stabling together at the competitions, in turn making it inevitable for Bern and Julie to become close. (Bern's father, Jim, was the brother of Julie's mother, Tanya.)

Julie was almost the same age as Bern (forty) and had never married. She was horse crazy, for sure. In fact, she might have been one of the very few women who was horse crazy without being just plain crazy, too. He'd owe her one if she could get him his girl. She certainly wasn't the type who expected to be rewarded but that proved how grateful he would be. Not to get ahead of himself, but it wasn't too early to start thinking about what it might be. Maybe he could play matchmaker for her, despite her resolve she was "happily single." No one really was.

***

Heather was a lucky girl. She had to be, if only because she always seemed to get what she wanted, not that she was spoiled. She worked hard, which said a lot in and of itself because she was only seventeen. Her parents gave her the freedom to take up riding and showing horses but never let her get carried away with it, such as buying her any horses. She had to prove herself to horse owners who might be interested in letting her show their mounts.

The last four years Heather had been homeschooled by her mother, Maggie, which coincided with when their family moved to Delaplane, Indiana, from Mesa, Arizona. Heather's father, Harold, had been transferred because of his job, which involved designing stuff. Heather wasn't sure exactly what, but they seemed to live pretty comfortably. Her parents probably could have afforded to buy her a horse or two, but anymore Heather was grateful they never did because she'd gained a lot more riding experience over the years than she otherwise would have. Riding a wide variety of horses had

Letter to Sarah

certainly boosted her confidence, although it didn't exactly translate to her personal life, in which she was painfully shy. It was one reason she had been homeschooled once the move to Indiana was made. Sometimes Heather felt like her parents were messing her up by being so protective of her.

When Heather was told by Julie, the lady she worked for, her cousin was looking for a rider for the summer, she was ready to say she wanted the job, despite knowing nothing about the guy. It was already a given, Heather was going to be allowed to take a summer break and work for a trainer. The fact Julie's cousin's stable was only an hour away, would be especially enticing for Heather's parents. They could drive Heather there and meet the trainer, only dropping her off if they were completely comfortable with the situation. Heather (and her parents) had known Julie the entire four years the former had been living in Delaplane, and she (Julie) was entirely trustworthy, which meant her cousin had to be, too. Therefore, sending him a video of Heather riding, was a must. Heather had proceeded to saddle up "Minty," a bay Thoroughbred whose owner paid the board but never showed up to ride him. Julie had told her to warm him up for a couple minutes and then she would shoot the video. It was perfect weather for riding, as the first of June generally was around here, unlike where she'd lived in Arizona.

Admittedly, Heather was kind of "afraid" of what lay ahead in her life, but the next step appeared to be striking out on her own a little bit and no longer always being under her parents' watchful eye(s). Although she had competed at shows in the Southwest, she never traveled far enough to be away from home for more than a night or two. She was always chaperoned by the trainer of the stable she was riding for, provided it was a woman. If the trainer was a man, his wife came along. Going to this new place would be a whole different set of circumstances, but she felt ready, despite being socially inept.

It had been very convenient having her parents "take care

of her," Heather was willing to allow. She didn't even have a driver's license! She walked to Julie's stable, as the driveway leading to her barn was only about 150 yards away. It was even on the same side of the street! Hopefully the trainer she wanted to work for, would be willing to drive her to the store once in awhile. Lodging was already taken care of because he had a studio guesthouse on the property. The setup would be even more convenient than what Heather had now, working for Julie. She really was lucky.

***

Shady Cove Stable had many pluses, but its location (a mere block from Shady Cove Lake) was what allowed the sixty-acre property to not only hold its value but appreciate. Once Bern finally left the area (he expected to inherit his dad's place up near the Illinois-Wisconsin state line), he hoped to get a minimum of three million for it, and that would be from a developer who would come in and bulldoze most of the buildings. In the meantime, he kept the place up as well as he could, considering he was always short-handed and riding the horses and going to shows was more important than keeping the property pristine. He was proud of the fact he had his priorities in order.

Another plus as far as the location of Bern's farm was its relative proximity to his cousin Julie's stable in Delaplane. Julie's neighbor/employee, Heather Turner, was coming up here to ride for him! Heather's parents were bringing her in a couple days, so he needed to clean the house and prepare the guesthouse, including putting silverware in there, including some sharp (in more ways than one) steak knives. He preferred using plastic utensils, and Michaela should have taken the silverware with her since the set had been a wedding gift. Anyway, the three of them were going to visit with Bern and make the final decision at that time. If the girl was anything to look at (not to mention resembled his ex), it would be difficult to maintain his composure! He looked forward to the challenge, however.

The tentative time frame was for Heather to stay two months. Hopefully she'd volunteer to remain here longer than that (as in "forever"). Bern was lonely just thinking about having to live a couple more days, all alone. She wasn't going to move in with him per se, but the guesthouse was only about seventy-five yards from the main house, separated by an in-ground pool. It was one amenity he maintained because nothing beat a swim after riding horses on a hot summer's day. A rich advertising mogul had built the houses and barns in the 1930s, when the area was less populated. The man had owned an apartment in Chicago and Shady Cove Stable was his getaway. It was called something else then, however. The main house was splendid in its heyday but needed some remodeling. Nonetheless, it was still classy and comfortable. One thing it was missing was a canine companion or two, as Bern's last dog passed away about a year ago. He seemed to stay so busy he almost didn't notice, although the lack of female company wasn't lost on him. He'd even occasionally wished his ex would return, simultaneously aware that was impossible (or so he thought).

***

Riding in the backseat of her father's red Toyota Camry, Heather was being driven by him (with her mother in the front passenger seat) to Shady Cove Stable, to meet Bern Wahler. She only had "talk and text" on her phone, so she couldn't search for a picture of the trainer online, should one exist. Admittedly she hadn't even thought about his looks until she happened to text a friend, Nicole, in Arizona, telling her what was going on. Heather was never that close to her, but they had stayed in touch ever since Heather's move to Indiana. If anything the distance made them communicate more than they otherwise would have. Nicole was in the same grade as Heather, so she too would be graduating soon. It was still very early in Arizona, so Nicole had a few minutes to text back and forth, keeping Heather engaged while trying to ignore her parents. They were listening to a talk radio show that was turned up quite loudly, so she couldn't hear exactly what they were saying. Or maybe she was subconsciously trying not to. Anyway, after Nicole had asked Heather what the trainer looked like and the latter admitted she didn't know, Nicole next asked if the guy was married! Heather thought that question was irrelevant and texted back: "What does that have to do with anything?"

Nicole replied: "DUH!"

Heather never was so proud to have been homeschooled. Nicole's remark indicated how an eighteen-year-old turned out, who went to public school. Not only was Heather finished with high school she was only seventeen! Since she was smarter than Nicole, rather than start a snippy exchange, Heather merely signed off with: "I'll let you know when I find out the guy's marital status and if he's cute."

Nicole texted in return: "For your sake you better hope he's married and on a tight leash!"

Heather doubted her parents would allow her to spend two months working for Bern Wahler if they had any reservations about him. Since he was Julie's cousin, he had to be a decent person. Heather couldn't help returning to this thought! If he wasn't, she would be really upset, although she wasn't sure how she would react.

Because Heather and her parents were originally from Arizona and had yet to visit the northern half of their new home state, they were seeing the area for the first time. The radio was still on, but they were finally silent. Heather hadn't realized how distracting it was, having them talk at the same time their favorite radio personality was blabbing. What Heather would have given to have driven up here by herself! It occurred to her, she could have gotten her license by this time, although it had always seemed enjoyable to be driven everywhere. Being at her parents' mercy suddenly made her so restless she could hardly stand it.

***

Bern was so nervous! The imminent visit from his prospective assistant and her parents was doing it. He'd even checked himself in the mirror several times in the last few minutes, to make sure he looked as good as he suspected he did. Originally he was going wear khakis and an open dress shirt (white or light blue) to meet the Turners, but he decided wearing his riding clothes (beige breeches, a navy polo shirt and boots) was more appropriate for the occasion.

One issue that needed to be discussed was whether or not Heather expected to receive a salary. He imagined she would be happy to working in exchange for a place to sleep and free meals, especially since most of her "work" would involve riding! The experience would be great for her resume, as she supposedly wanted to train horses for a living. She had the talent, or so it appeared, given what Bern saw of her riding thus far, but did she have the temperament? One thing you needed was a thick skin, and he wasn't referring to being protected when you fell off.

Bern was looking out the kitchen window when "she" exited the backseat of a red Toyota Camry, her body like a yearling's, her legs still too long for her overly- slim body . . . There was plenty of exquisiteness to take in before looking at her face! When he finally did, he couldn't believe the likeness to his ex-wife's.

It was assumed Heather had arrived with a suitcase or two, but no one made a move to extricate anything from the trunk. Instead her parents got out of the car and headed straight for the front door, Heather behind them. They appeared somewhat tentative, as it was possible they were slightly apprehensive about the situation, now that they were here.

Amy Kristoff

Bern decided the best thing to do was go outside and greet them, rather than stand in the house, waiting for one of them to knock on the rustic wood front door. He proceeded to open it (he never noticed until this moment, how loudly it creaked) and introduced himself once he was standing on the flagstone stoop. Mr. and Mrs. Turner shook hands with Bern first and then Heather finally made eye contact with Bern when they shook hands. Her father proceeded to introduce her as "my lovely daughter, Heather." Indeed she was.

Heather's eyes were green, and they seemed to look right through Bern, which was very disconcerting. He had expected to fall in love with her at first sight, and even though she was young, he'd anticipated she would at least be receptive to him. It was possible he'd never get much of anywhere with her, not in two months. And he hated waiting for anything. Another plan was in order.

The four of them sat down in what Bern called "the front room," which was actually a porch that had been enclosed and had a painted concrete floor with a colorful throw rug. There were two brown wicker loveseats and a matching wicker rocking chair, which had bamboo-print cushions. Bern seated himself in the rocking chair. One loveseat was very close to the rocking chair, and it happened to be where Heather was expected to sit, as her parents had seated themselves first, across from him. When Bern spoke to them, she had a close, unobstructed view of him, making him self-conscious! Why had he ever thought he was up to the task of seducing a young girl? He suddenly felt like an old man. He was only a few years younger, at the most, than Heather's father. As it was, Bern was doing a lot of assuming regarding Heather working for him, especially if he couldn't appear likable and trustworthy!

Bern's cousin Julie was one person who possessed those two attributes. She truly was an inspiration and Bern wished he could be more like her. He started the conversation with the Turners by explaining how close he was to Julie when

Letter to Sarah

they were growing up and how appreciative he was of her being their "liaison." Immediately afterward Bern wanted to put his foot (boot and all) in his mouth for having said that. Instead he ploughed ahead and proceeded to ask any one of the three, what Heather had been paid, working for his cousin.

Mr. Turner replied, "I'm not sure what Heather is paid an hour, but here she just wants to soak up your expertise, Bern. At Julie's she cleans stalls and whatnot, not that she couldn't here, but she would like to concentrate on riding as much as possible, with plenty of supervision from you, whatever your schedule will allow, insofar as one-on-one time alone with her."

"She certainly will be able to ride a lot here and I'd be more than happy to help her," Bern told him. "I already have people to clean stalls and feed, even when I'm at a show and take help with me. So the bottom line is she doesn't have to be bothered with any chores. It probably looks like I don't even have any help on a day like today because Monday is an 'off' day. Jerome feeds morning and evening and that's about it."

"I like all the barn work, no matter what it is," Heather stated, looking hard at Bern. "And Julie paid me nine dollars an hour, cash. Lots of times I even got a little extra if I stayed late to hold horses for the farrier, stuff like that."

Suffice to mention Bern "got it" and vaguely nodded, although there was nothing "vague" regarding what he was thinking. He wished she wasn't so attractive yet difficult overall to "read." Again, it was imperative to have patience. He needed to concentrate on the fact she wanted to work! If one of Bern's employees, Jerome or anyone else, didn't show up to work (which happened quite often), it was a safe bet he could count on Heather to fill in. He ought to be grateful if she stayed on for the two months and provided extra help, not obsess over wanting something beyond a platonic relationship with her.

Amy Kristoff

After chatting with Mr. and Mrs. Turner for a couple more minutes, Bern was certain they had no idea the impression their gorgeous daughter made on a middle-aged man, living alone. The situation compelled Bern to both laugh and cry: the former because of their cluelessness, the latter because their equally naïve daughter would be the one paying the price. Perhaps, however, he was wrong about Heather, as her apparent shyness was instead insolence. The fact she was hard to figure out really intrigued him. He imagined she had zero sexual experience, something he wasn't supposed to be pondering but couldn't help it!

It was decided Heather would initially work "for free," but Bern would give her spending money if what her parents sent her, wasn't enough for her basic needs. He started to mention something about the cook he had three days a week, but then they would think he was super-rich. If he could avoid paying someone who would be exercising his horses, he was all for it! He intended to help her, but he had other things in mind when he thought of "helping."

Before any final decision was made as to whether or not Heather would be working at Shady Cove Stable, Mr. Turner announced the three of them were going to grab a bite to eat and talk about it. Bern recommended they stop in at "The Lighthouse," which was only a couple miles down the road and was right on Shady Cove Lake, appropriately enough. He just hoped if he was told "no" regarding Heather taking the position, the whole family didn't return here to tell him – a phone call would suffice, preferably from Mr. Turner.

It was going to be a long forty-five minutes to an hour while Bern awaited "the verdict." It was funny he used that term to describe what he assumed was the Turners' collective decision regarding if Heather would be spending the next two months riding for him. Maybe he had it all wrong and she made the final decision on her own. Still, her parents' input was to be expected.

Letter to Sarah

***

At The Lighthouse Heather ordered a chef's salad and a Coke while her parents both ordered club sandwiches with French fries and diet Cokes. She sipped her soft drink and listened to them discuss the man she was possibly going to ride horses for. They kept bringing up the fact Bern Wahler seemed a little too eager to have Heather on board, which she formerly would have determined was "overreacting." However, given what Nicole had texted earlier about Bern's potential motives, maybe they were onto something for a change. As mentioned, Heather knew her father designed stuff and it was for a heavy machinery company, which sounded impressive, but neither one of her parents had ever impressed her, insofar as being "smart" or "with it." Granted, Heather's mother had home-schooled her for four years, but that didn't exactly blow Heather away.

If Bern decided to put the moves on Heather, that would be really awful. He was actually quite handsome, but he was so much older than herself! She was a long way from thinking "like that" about him. She had yet to even go on a real date with a boy close to her own age! Hopefully Bern wasn't assuming anything just by looking at her because she really wanted to work at his stable but that was it.

She guessed the best thing to do was never go in his house. It was impossible he'd barge in the guesthouse and force himself on her while she was sleeping. He seemed too mannerly for something like that. Besides, word would get back to Julie, and he'd look like an idiot or worse. Julie would be even angrier than Heather's parents.

While Heather continued to try and think of Bern in another way besides a man who trained horses, her parents had concluded he was an O.K. guy, when all was said and done. Therefore, if Heather wanted to spend two months at his place, that was O.K., too. It was assumed Heather was waiting for these O.K.s because she was already 100% sold on him. Also, if she changed her mind about staying at any point before the two months was up, her parents were only an hour away and could pick her up. It certainly sounded like a reassuring option.

Heather wished she were allowed to bring her phone into restaurants. She would have texted Nicole and told her what was up—and that Bern was "pretty cute." (She supposed he was, for a forty-some-year-old man.) However, it had not been confirmed if he was married. Nicole would scold her for not knowing for sure, so it was better anyway to wait to contact her, possibly not for two months. The whole adventure was going to be Heather's "personal and private surprise." That sounded so cool she had to smile. Her parents took absolutely no notice.

Lunch soon arrived, so the Turner family occupied themselves with eating. Heather was slightly bothered by the fact neither one of her parents was inclined to discuss even one aspect of Bern Wahler with her, such as what she should do "in case." If a total stranger had asked her if she trusted people in general, she would have replied she had no reason not to, especially since she was still young. Or maybe it had to do with how lucky she was.

***

Michaela Wahler had made an enormous mistake when she divorced her husband, Bern, having done so because he barely paid attention to her! What little time they did spend together, they got along fine, although they admittedly had nothing in common. Based solely on the fact she was above-average in looks, Michaela had expected to remarry without a problem. It turned out not every man was interested in a divorcee, even if she was still attractive. Actually her appearance worked against her because men figured she was divorced and childless because she was "difficult" in whatever capacity. Who in his right mind wanted to delve into find-

Letter to Sarah

ing out exactly what made her "difficult"?

In a word, Michaela was MISERABLE. Also, she missed her ex's cavernous house that she swore was haunted (but it didn't bother her). However, she had to get used to it before being able to make that declaration. Her favorite room was the enclosed porch, if only because it was the only room that had newer furniture, albeit wicker. She left the two wicker loveseats and the rocking chair behind, along with the cushions so Bern could have something in the house that didn't look completely dated. He'd claim since he was barely in the house, it didn't matter what the furniture looked like – and he was chintzy about giving Michaela money to buy something new. She realized she must have loved him even more than she was aware, to have put up with that kind of attitude, not that it was an actual hardship. Then again, at times it appeared to be just that because it was no fun sitting alone on musty old furniture in a big, creepy house. She also left the wedding gift silverware set, which was regretful (in ways she couldn't imagine).

It was decided (at least for Michaela): she was going back to Bern and beg him to let her live with him. They didn't even have to remarry. Given the amount of time since she left (four years already!) the possibility existed he was with someone new. If that was the case, she'd pretend to be passing through and stopped by to say hello, on her way to the Wisconsin Dells from Indianapolis, her first vacation in years. Given how hard Bern had taken their divorce it was possible he wouldn't want to see her ever again. She would have attempted to reach out to him via social media, but he wasn't into that at all and was in fact a pretty uncomplicated guy, which she missed. He was obsessed with horses, so what? At least she didn't have to be too concerned about him cheating on her, definitely not emotionally (such as online).

Although Michaela never was a "night person," she ended up becoming a bartender at an upscale Indianapolis area hotel to support herself. Actually she had been one way back when, so it was the first occupation to return to, given her familiarity with it. The only aspect she enjoyed about it was the tips. It wasn't the right job through which to find her next husband if only because she didn't drink. However, some of the men she served undoubtedly had money, which never failed to provide allure.

If Michaela was given another chance with Bern, she vowed to finally ride, although she would have to force herself not to be afraid of horses (including when sitting on one). Bern never had one that was slow and plodding enough, as they were athletes, bred for jumping competitions. The few shows she'd attended with him, the only activity she'd enjoyed was socializing after the showing was over for the day.

As much as Michaela enjoyed Bern's company, he was always on the go. She was much more laid-back. They must have balanced one another out better than she thought because she'd been bored out of her mind ever since she was no longer with him. Bern had to take her back, that was all there was to it. Even though he didn't keep in close contact with his cousin, Julie (that Michaela was aware), maybe it was beneficial to get in touch with her (Julie). Bern thought the world of his cousin and perhaps she'd be willing to put in a good word for Michaela, not that Julie owed her anything.

***

Heather thought she had a pretty comfortable bed at home, but this one in the guesthouse at Bern's was a lot better. For one thing it was queen-sized and hers was full-sized. The pillows were noticeably denser than the ones she was used to, which made laying her head on them all the more relaxing. If she complained about the pillows her mother would tell her to buy her own. When Heather returned home, she would. Her mother would have to drive her someplace to buy them, was all.

Letter to Sarah

The fact Heather wasn't more responsible and hadn't gotten out and lived more was her own doing. Neither one of her parents had told her she couldn't get a driver's license or date, it was a matter of neither one bothering to suggest she do so. Had she purposely hobbled herself? It was an important question because she might in turn be harboring some hidden anger issues.

Maybe Shady Cove Stable didn't feel so isolated when there were other workers around. Bern said he had two full-time grooms besides the guy who fed the horses on Mondays. There was another man who did mostly yard maintenance and handyman chores, but he ran his own business too so he wasn't around all the time. Bern said he tried every year to do some yardwork himself but never got around to it. He'd rather clean stalls if need be. Heather had reiterated her willingness to help with any chores, and once she was busy all day the time would (hopefully) fly by. It already seemed like forever since she had lunch with her parents, and that was earlier in the day! She regretted having felt irritated by their presence. The fact Bern's property wasn't remote, made it all the more strange. There was plenty of privacy, however, making Heather ill-at-ease. She was particularly uncomfortable in a new place if she couldn't see anything outside the door after dark. There was one security light on the other side of the main house as well as one in front of the barn, but the latter was at least a hundred yards away. There was a carriage light on a pole in front of the guesthouse, but it either didn't work or the bulb was burned out. Tomorrow morning Heather would ask Bern if he could have his maintenance guy take a look at it. She'd even explain why, if need be!

One thing Heather wished she'd brought along was her bicycle. It wasn't much, but it would have been useful for riding to not-too-distant downtown Shady Cove. Walking would take too much time, although she'd prefer that to asking Bern for a ride. Now that she was in this living arrangement, she was (finally) wary. He hadn't made a pass at her, but she was starting think it was only a matter of time. Nicole would have laughed if she knew what Heather was regretting: not going right back home! Heather would call her parents in the morning and have them pick her up if she still didn't feel right about staying here. That suggestion calmed her, although it was difficult to fall asleep, and she kept changing positions.

***

She was beautiful, even more so when asleep, "she" being Heather, of course. It was a good thing Bern had the farm memorized, inside and outside, because the studio guesthouse was nearly dark and the one lousy light in front didn't work. She was completely out, or she would have sat up and started screaming at some point. He must have been leaning over her for a good five minutes, which was like eternity when you feared "getting caught" the whole time! She was lucky he didn't drink or do drugs, or he would have done something stupid by this point. (It was lost on Bern, he was doing anything wrong, standing here.)

Bern had to leave when he started considering the what-ifs, particularly if he hadn't installed central air in the guesthouse a few years ago: Heather would have most likely been sleeping on top of the bed and possibly would have been in the nude. The mere thought was almost too much!

Exiting via the side door, passing the kitchen area, Bern made sure to lock the door on his way out. He wouldn't have wanted to give himself away by failing to leave the door unlocked. He wanted to make a habit of this if he would so choose. It was more titillating than he imagined, yet he didn't have to give away what a weirdo he really was! He would have a hard time not coming back again before the night was over.

***

Letter to Sarah

Heather did her best to remain calm when Bern was leaning over her while she was trying to sleep. It was just as well she'd been tossing and turning before he'd shown up, unlocking the side door to enter, versus entering via the front door, which opened upon the sitting area, with a ragged-looking sofa and an ancient TV on a round coffee table, in the corner. The best feature was the polished oak floor throughout. Had she been sound asleep when he'd come in the house, she would have been startled awake and then screamed. Instead she'd lain very still and breathed evenly, telling herself if she panicked, he might panic too and who knew what he might do to shut her up? It was possible he'd "accidentally" strangle her.

Even if Bern never again visited like he just did, Heather was 100% done with this experience. He was a major creep-o. Her parents might not believe her when she told them what happened, so it was tempting to leave her suitcase and start walking home, taking matters into her own hands. Anything to get out of spending the rest of the night here. Maybe she should walk to the police station. There had to be one in downtown Shady Cove. She couldn't call anyone because her phone was dead. Perhaps she could make an emergency call, but was she technically in any danger or just weirded-out? If she knew for sure Bern wouldn't return anymore for the night, she could at least get some sleep. She was so upset her mind was going in every direction.

Heather finally came up with what seemed like a doable plan: she would stick it out for the night after all, and in the meantime her phone would be charging. She'd call home first thing in the morning and tell her parents she was extremely sick, and she wouldn't say a word about Bern's behavior. They wouldn't leave her here if they thought she might need to be admitted to the hospital. One thing she'd never done was fake an illness, so if she said she was sick, they'd believe her.

No sooner had Heather almost dozed off when she heard

Amy Kristoff

a key being inserted in the side door lock. With the headboard of the bed against the wall opposite to the kitchen area, there was a short distance to the kitchen cabinets. Bern had shown her where he'd placed a new-looking silverware set, which included some kick-ass steak knives. He said he couldn't use the utensils because they reminded him of his failed marriage. She'd grab one of those knives and make him pay.

No One Winner

Every summer the Lake County Fair in Harmony, Indiana, was a popular draw. It was amazing, in the age of technology, so many people still cared about "the simpler things in life." Even the more recent residents of the area, many of whom lived in upscale subdivisions, spent at least part of a day at the fairgrounds. There was in fact a newer, affluent subdivision, "Fairview," across Fairview Street (both appropriately named), on the west side of the fairgrounds. Formerly fair attendees parked where four and five-thousand square-foot residences now stood, as it was once a hay field. A week before the fair started (the first Friday in August), signs would go up at the entrance to the subdivision, warning fair goers not to park beyond that point or anywhere along Fairview Street. The east, north, and south sides of the fairgrounds had either businesses or well-established neighborhoods (older, modest-looking houses), and "No Parking" signs during the ten days of the fair, were harder to find, due to being unnecessary, for whatever reason.

A resident of Fairview since 2013, Dolores Chambers (her husband was Dr. Charles Chambers, M.D.) attempted to initiate a petition to have the fair phased out by the year 2020. She figured if she got everyone's signature who lived in "her" subdivision, that would suffice, given what everyone paid each year in property taxes. One problem was she couldn't get anyone to sign the petition. Just the fact Charles' and her Georgian Colonial faced Fairview Street, Dolores' biggest peeve was the lights from inside the fairgrounds "blasted

Amy Kristoff

through all the front windows of the house, both floors," for more than just the ten days of the fair, given the time before and after, when workers were setting up and then taking down the amusement park rides and displays. The house was actually on Teller Street, set back from Fairview by a hundred feet, with landscaping in between Teller and Fairview. (All the common area maintenance within Fairview subdivision was paid for through the homeowner's association.) In a few years, hopefully the fir trees and honeysuckle bushes would finally grow enough to block out some of the invasive light. It was an issue even with the blinds closed.

Another dilemma was the noise, and Dolores was not only referring to the general din, but the music concert the first Friday of the fair, as well as another one the next night and the following Saturday, too. The second Friday evening had a monster truck pull, and on the final night, Sunday, there was a fireworks display.

When Dolores and Charles were deciding whether to purchase their house, it was the dead of winter. They were aware of the fair taking place every August but had figured it was "only a week," which turned out to be a conservative assumption. The real estate agent helping the builder sell the home had cheerfully offered, "You could always take a trip that week, get away from it all." They had done so on one occasion, and they'd had to come back early because Dolores had an unbearable toothache and refused to go to anyone but her regular dentist.

Last year was probably the most tolerable of the years Dolores and Charles had had to "endure the fair" (how Dolores referred to what she went through, truth be told). It rained like crazy five of the ten days, which didn't shut the fair down completely those days, but two of the concerts were cancelled. Also, the fireworks show was nixed because Mother Nature had provided her own light and sound show for the grand finale that Sunday evening. In fact there was a power outage for almost an hour because of a lightning

Letter to Sarah

strike. Dolores was never so thrilled to sit in the dark. Charles had been on call at the hospital, as St. Anthony's was barely a mile away, to the southeast of the fairgrounds. He took things in stride more so than she, and his "line of work" enabled him to keep things in perspective.

Fortunately, now that the grandkids (Janie, 11, and Kyle, 10) were finally "getting older," one would finally be providing some entertainment, versus merely needing a babysitter. This would be the first year Janie was going to be in a horse show at the fair. Next year Kyle would be exhibiting an animal in 4-H, once it was decided what animal would be the most suitable. Dolores was excited for them both and in turn was attempting to adopt a favorable attitude toward the fair. Neither grandchild could have suspected what Dolores really thought of the fairgrounds and everything about it, although Janie was quite perceptive, not unlike her mother, Jane.

Speaking of Jane, having grown up in a "staid" (boring) household, she had evidently been compelled to find a challenging hobby. She'd wanted a horse since she was very young and wanted to compete on him in the Olympics. Dolores had initially found her only child's infatuation with horses annoying, but as Jane got older and her obsession with horses wasn't replaced with an obsession with boys, Dolores finally regarded horses with some appreciation. Although Jane's dream of riding in the Olympics was but a fantasy, at least she was driven. Dolores nearly envied her at times, as she herself had no drive at all.

The Chambers family had formerly lived in an established, upscale Chicago suburb where there were a number of horse boarding and training stables from which to choose for Jane's initiation to riding. Dolores knew absolutely nothing about horses and the riding/training protocol. She picked "Oak Mount Stable" in Lake Forest, on a recommendation from her sister, Rachel, who had recently taken her daughter, Carmen, there for "jumping lessons." Neither one knew anything about horses or riding, just like Dolores and

Amy Kristoff

Jane. Oak Mount's trainer, Cristy Little, said Carmen would need her own horse because she didn't have any "lesson horses." Cristy had some horses for sale but nothing was less than fifteen thousand dollars. Rachel really liked the trainer, as did Carmen, but that was too much money for a horse. Nonetheless, Rachel told Dolores about the experience, aware Jane wanted to take up riding and eventually compete at jumping shows, like Carmen had wanted to do. Also, she knew Dolores and her husband wouldn't be deterred by the price tag of fifteen thousand (or more) for a horse.

At barely thirteen, Jane ended up being allowed to purchase a warmblood cross gelding (whose stable name was "Mighty") from Cristy and was soon jumping him, despite having never spent any time in the saddle prior to owning him. She was either extremely talented or very lucky. Jane campaigned Mighty in the large junior hunters by the following summer and did so through her final year of eligibility (age 18). She sold him after the last show she attended at the end of July and got almost as much as her parents paid for him, despite his advancing years. He went to a good home, so she didn't have to worry about his welfare.

After attending Southern Illinois University- Carbondale and earning a teaching degree, Jane returned home, but she was anxious to have her own place – and she wanted it to be horse property, in the Chicagoland area. Luckily she was able to get a teaching job south of the city, as she never could have afforded a property where she grew up. That was how she ended up buying a ten-acre farm in Crete. Despite the modest price of the property (the whole place needed a lot of work), Dolores thought for sure she and Charles were going to have to swoop in and help their daughter financially. Not long after moving in (Jane didn't mind enduring the condition of the house while it was slowly remodeled), she re-connected with a high school boyfriend, Kevin, who had moved to the area as well (and was renting a place) and worked for his brother's excavating business. She fell in love (or re-fell

Letter to Sarah

in love?) with him and got married. Not only that she supplemented her income by working for her brother-in-law on the weekends, doing bookkeeping and organizing his office. And she still found time to ride her two new horses.

Dolores and Charles did an excellent job of raising their daughter (and bestowed upon her good genes) and both were proud of her. Dolores just wished he'd been around more (versus at work).

***

Jane was ambivalent about her daughter, Janie, having taken up riding because she was compelled to be her trainer, at least for another year. At the same time, maybe being her daughter's trainer was selfish on her (Jane's) part.

When Jane had originally become interested in horses, what she would have given to have had her mother be a rider too! Jane hadn't even gotten any encouragement, at least not at first. It was largely thanks to Jane's one and only trainer, Cristy Little, she, Jane, was allowed to buy a horse. In other words, it had taken forever for Jane's mother to warm up to the idea of Jane riding, yet once they both met Cristy, things started to really happen. That was all Jane could conclude regarding her mother's change in attitude. Jane had her aunt Rachel to thank because she had looked up Cristy as a trainer for her daughter, Carmen (who ended up playing tennis instead of taking riding lessons).

Jane had vowed she would never be anything but encouraging toward whatever her kids decided to do, no lag time allowed. Her husband, Kevin, was the same way. Also, he was interested in their kids' doings, unlike Jane's father was with her, mostly because he worked so much. It was fortunate Jane and Kevin had zero disputes about how to raise their two kids. Otherwise there would have been a lot of arguments.

The horse Janie currently had, "Oro," a grade, palomino

Amy Kristoff

Quarter Horse gelding, was from a local trainer, Sandy Mertz. Jane had been to the woman's stable a few times over the years, to look at horses she'd had for sale. Sandy appeared knowledgeable but probably didn't know a whole lot more than Jane did. Jane knew of a couple other trainers in the area who offered lessons, but they were men, and she wasn't sure if Janie would be comfortable under their tutelage. (Or was Jane thinking of herself?)

The supposed story on Oro (his stable name) was the (former) owner had quit paying her horse's board for over a year, so Sandy exercised the right to claim the horse as her own, per the terms of the boarding contract her attorney-husband drafted. Once the horse was legally declared Sandy's, naturally she offered him for sale. As a supposedly unregistered Quarter Horse, he wasn't very big, which was perfect for Janie as she learned the basics. Not a word was ever mentioned how the former owner of Oro, felt about having surrendered ownership of her horse. Possibly circumstances beyond her control, kept her from being able to pay the board a couple of months, yet it appeared on paper, it was longer than that or there were other issues. Jane didn't question the circumstances, nor did she ever tell Janie any of the (purported) backstory on Oro. Janie loved her horse! They trusted one another more and more, so their performance at the fair would demonstrate how much progress they'd made in their year-long relationship. It would in fact be only the fourth show they'd attended together, although Oro had a lengthy show record (so it was claimed), having formerly participated in many all-breed competitions. Nonetheless, the show ring at the Lake County Fairgrounds was daunting, even for a seasoned competitor, horse or rider.

***

The show was coming up on Monday. After one last lesson on Saturday, Janie said she was ready and felt like Oro was, too. She would give him a bath on Sunday afternoon, and afterward Jane would help her load the trailer with the necessary tack and other equipment. Janie's brother, Kyle, didn't want to go because he would have "nothing to do." Jane told him he had to go so he could look at all the exhibits and animals in order to decide for sure what he wanted to show in 4-H next year (pending his parents' final approval). Obviously he wasn't interested in horses, but some of his disinterest might have been because his sister liked them. The two siblings got along reasonably well, but they didn't like to appear to be copying one another.

Jane would have said her mother wouldn't have moved to Indiana for anything, but Jane's father joined a general practice that included a couple former colleagues, within the nearby hospital. He also filled in in the emergency room "as needed." He detested driving anywhere, so even the fifteen-minute trip to the Illinois-Indiana state line would have caused him to complain, and there was no guarantee he and Jane's mother would have found something to their liking, anyway. If it hadn't been for the existence of the subdivision where they found their dream house, they might have remained in Lake Forest, although Jane's father sincerely wanted to leave both the area and the hospital where he had practiced. One thing was for certain: Jane's mother never would have tolerated living across from the Lake County Fairgrounds if it wasn't in an impressive-looking house. Simply put: Jane's mother was not humble. Living where Jane's parents did, was a compromise for them both.

***

Dolores never could have griped there wasn't easy access to the fairgrounds from her front door; a walk-in entrance was located directly across Fairview Street. It was a leftover from the days when patrons parked in the former hay field. She found it ironic, paying money to gain access to a place she wished would cease to exist.

Jane had said she would be parking her truck and trailer in a designated spot that probably wouldn't be particularly close to the show ring. Therefore, it was recommended Dolores look for Jane and the kids near the adjacent warm-up area, of which two sides were enclosed by wooden snow fence. The north side, which was the closest to the stabling and parking areas, was completely open. The east side met up with the show ring, which was enclosed by four boards of PVC fencing. Janie was riding in the second class of the afternoon, the first one to begin at 1:00 p.m. It was about ten until the hour, and it was a pretty humid day. Although Dolores had thought wearing white leather, strapless sandals was a good idea when she left the house, she no longer felt that way. It was just that they were the only shoes that looked good with her white capri pants and black-and-white striped, three-quarter-sleeved, linen top. From what she'd seen thus far, she was the only one not dressed like a slob.

By the time Dolores reached the set of bleachers closest to the warm-up area and in-gate, she had already passed countless food and souvenir stands, including one that customized vehicle plates. She contemplated purchasing one that had a colorful sunset and having it personalized with her name. That would have looked neat on the front of her royal blue Escalade. Instead she bought a Mountain Dew fountain drink and headed for a seat.

No one was yet sitting by the in-gate on the south side of the ring, so Dolores had her choice of places. However, some riders were milling around the warm-up area, and an announcement had been made for the first class: "Beginner Walk-Trot, Ten and Under, Ponies." After Dolores looked around and confirmed Janie had not yet made an appearance, she turned to plop down on the lowest bleachers. Before doing so, she realized white was the wrong color of capri pants to have worn here. Why hadn't she thought her outfit through a little better? She happened to have taken a

Letter to Sarah

couple napkins when she bought her soda, so she used them to attempt to wipe off some of the dirt where she intended to sit. Carefully she finally sat down.

An announcement was made regarding the entrants for the first class: they would be allowed to enter the ring at a walk, going counter-clockwise. Dolores looked up and past the warm-up ring, to see Janie on her horse, slowly walking him down the hill from the stabling and parking areas, Jane to the horse's left, Kyle to the right. The name of the horse continued to elude her—and he was indeed a horse, although not a big one.

Jane didn't appear to be looking for Dolores in the bleachers, which was understandable, as she was busy keeping an eye on Janie and her mount. However, it didn't seem as if Jane had any reason for concern, since the horse looked completely calm. Janie was wearing a black, hunt-style helmet, beige breeches, a navy coat and black boots. Dolores pulled out her digital camera and took a picture, even though they were still quite far away and she made no adjustments for such a long shot. She decided to stay put until after Janie's class in order to avoid distracting her.

By this time all the entrants for the first class were in the ring, but the gate was still open. Suddenly a woman appeared from the left side of the warm-up area, pointing at Janie and her horse and yelling, "Moby! Moby! Moby!" Then she darted left, heading for the one open side of the warm-up area.

Approaching Janie and her horse (and Jane and Kyle) from behind, the woman exclaimed, "Excuse me! That happens to be my horse! He might as well have been stolen from me, given what Sandy Mertz and her shit-lawyer husband did to me!"

The woman's histrionics had finally garnered some stares, including from the man who had just shut the gate for the show ring. He walked up to her and told her no loitering was allowed in the warm-up ring, to which she retorted,

Amy Kristoff

"Then tell them to get away from the girl and 'her' horse, who happens to be my Moby." She was of course accusing Jane and Kyle of "loitering." A couple more riders had appeared for the second class ("Beginner Walk-Trot, Ten and Under, Horses"), and they were accompanied by "loiterers" too.

***

Jane was beside herself. Enough had already been said to make her regret having bought Oro from Sandy Mertz. The visibly upset woman standing before her had evidently been duped in some way, but the last person who deserved any blame was Janie. Therefore, couldn't the woman back off for a few minutes and let Janie ride Oro in their class?

Hopefully the woman skulked away, was what Jane kept thinking as she continued to stand beside Janie on Oro. Kyle had moved from the opposite side of Oro and was standing next to his mother. The riders in the ring had just reversed direction, so the first class was halfway over. That did not give Janie much time before she would be demonstrating her riding talent to the spectators of the Lake County Fair!

***

The announcer told the riders in the ring to line up their ponies facing the stabling area, having just slowed them from a trot to a walk. Given where Dolores was seated, she had the pleasure of looking at the backs of eight riders and their ponies' rumps, as they awaited the results.

It turned out every contestant "won," and each rider was handed a blue ribbon as she (and he) exited the arena. Dolores was frankly disappointed in the decision to make everyone in the class a winner, but maybe it was for the best —and Janie's class would most likely conclude in the same manner.

Dolores kept her vision locked on Janie and her horse as

Letter to Sarah

they entered the ring at a walk, counter-clockwise, per the request of the announcer. Meanwhile, Jane and Kyle had sat down on the bleachers directly opposite to the ones where Dolores was sitting. Who proceeded to sit down to Dolores' left but the woman who had rudely approached Janie and called her horse "Moby"! It was impossible for Dolores to keep her undivided attention on her granddaughter when she couldn't resist continually giving the woman accusatory looks!

By the time the ten horses and riders in the ring were first trotting, the woman couldn't help asking Dolores, "Is there a specific reason you're staring at me so much?"

"Yes there is, as a matter of fact," Dolores replied but held off elaborating.

"What is it?"

"I'm trying to memorize what a person looks like who's so inexplicably rude."

"How the flip do you come up with that for an excuse when you're rude yourself? Look in the mirror!"

"If I need to look in the mirror, you need to do some soul-searching someplace far, far away from here."

The final statement of Dolores' appeared to shut the woman up. Then Janie slowed her horse to a walk, per the instructions from the announcer. They happened to be almost even with Dolores, so she whipped out her camera and took a quick picture. Neither Janie nor her horse appeared to notice, but the woman sure did. Rather than utter a word, however, she got up and left. Good riddance to her, was all Dolores could think.

Party Time—Not!

The graduation party was going to be perfect. It had to be because nothing in the Shaker household wasn't, if only due to the matriarch, Nina, making sure of as much! That wasn't to say she was a helicopter parent, not by any means. If anything she hadn't been around as much as she should have been over the years for her daughter, Marcy. It was Nina's one and only regret, which was a pretty good record for someone pushing fifty. It was entirely impossible her "approach" to raising her daughter had any noticeable, long-term effects. Marcy graduated from Thunderbird High School yesterday, June 1st, "a year late." She had to repeat senior year because of so many absences. It just so happened Nina had to repeat eighth grade because a serious illness kept her home for a long stretch of time. Marcy didn't have a valid excuse, something that was inexcusable on her mother's part, too.

Supposedly Marcy's father (Nina's ex-husband) was coming to the party, which made sense. He would be ready to celebrate the fact he'd no longer have to pay Nina even one more dime in child support. However, it wasn't as if Marcy had the inclination to leap into the real world and get a full-time job, find a place to live, etc. Therefore, technically there wasn't too much to celebrate. Nonetheless, Nina was always up for a party because one never failed to put her in a good mood. Also, the backyard of her Phoenix home looked gorgeous when decorated. The in-ground pool always made a great backdrop for parties. In all truth Julian's presence could be

Letter to Sarah

a bit awkward, as Nina hadn't seen him in a couple years, nor had Marcy. He almost constantly traveled around the U.S. and occasionally abroad, lecturing on the relevancy of ancient philosophers in modern times. He was doing something right because he really raked in the cash and was obviously in great demand. Some of his success was thanks to his charisma. He was Midwest born and raised (the Columbus, Ohio area), but he had acquired a certain affectation over the years, undoubtedly somewhat due to his status. Nina no longer even knew the man she was once married to, but at least it kept her from missing him. He was always just a windbag to her, albeit a well-spoken one. However, she really did love him at one point. The fact he grew bored with her and their family remained what she resented most about him.

Possibly Julian's son, Stephen, would be coming to the party as well. He was from Julian's first marriage to Janna, a flight attendant. Nina had never asked him how those two met, but it must have started out as a fling because he'd confessed to being "horny and dumb" when he'd bedded her. Just like with Marcy, Julian lost interest in his son and was absent for most of Stephen's formative years. Apparently Stephen didn't hold it against his father and they got along great. At 42, Stephen was restless like his father, but at least he didn't fight it by marrying and/or having kids. He was an art appraiser for estates and auction houses, last Nina heard. He was probably staying with "Dad" for the weekend before heading off to his next assignment. Julian's home base was right here in Phoenix, where he owned a condominium. Coincidentally it was only a couple miles from her house, as the property was located in the Biltmore Estates. Rumor had it, despite the fact he constantly traveled, he resented the fact he no longer owned what he'd considered "his" house and was a sore loser about as much – to this day!

Could Nina have declared Marcy didn't resent having been ignored by her father for much of her upbringing? She honestly couldn't say for sure. The truth was about to come out (unless Julian was a no-show, which was entirely possible). Again, Julian's lack of apparent involvement with his daughter was concerning to Nina, although she should have been resigned by this time.

Nina was doing all the party decorating, cooking and preparing herself, since it would be a rather small get-together, to include only Marcy's co-workers at "Just Yogurt." No relatives would be in attendance. Both of Nina's parents had passed away and her sister lived on the East Coast with her husband and three kids, one of whom was graduating from college. Marcy had made this particular request for her "guest list," and Nina wanted it to be her daughter's day and no one else's. Therefore, she failed to consider the request a bit strange. Also, Nina was asked if arrangements could be made to have "Miss H." the psychic visit for an hour or two. Supposedly the woman was best friends with Just Yogurt's owner, Sami Shane, to the point Miss H. was allowed to leave her business cards in a glass holder by the cash register. Not only that she was supposedly "very accurate." Nina never noticed the business cards when she'd been in Just Yogurt but wished she'd picked one up because all she had to go on was the phone number of the psychic, given to her by an impatient Marcy. Of course Nina would make sure her daughter got her wish. Julian would disapprove of the mere presence of a psychic (if he showed up), as he'd consider that type of thing totally provincial. Stephen was probably as stuffy as his father and would agree. Nonetheless, Nina was "the queen of her castle," and it hadn't been easy wrangling the house and plenty of money from her ex, all so she could be set for life and not have to do anything all day!

Initially Nina hadn't minded the fact Marcy wanted all her co-workers to come to her graduation party. After all, Marcy had an excellent attendance record at work (unlike for school), not that it had any relevancy to the issue at hand. Unfortunately, Nina was having second thoughts about

Letter to Sarah

opening her house to strangers. Marcy didn't even know exactly how many of her co-workers would be coming ("five to ten" at last count). Many of them were part-timers, like herself, and were mere acquaintances. Nina was grateful her daughter was raised to be "inclusive" with people. However, it would be impossible to keep an eye on everyone without appearing paranoid. The party was supposed to start around two-thirty or three and be over by six. No alcohol would be served, and it was assumed no one would sneak in his or her own. Nina was not a drinker and since some guests would most likely be underage (not just Marcy), it was better to be even-handed. Also, it was said Just Yogurt participated in some sort of program to provide employment for ex-convicts. As much as Nina wanted everyone (former felons?) to stay in the pool area or under the covered patio, inevitably someone would end up wandering inside, especially if he or she decided it was hot out and didn't want to jump in the pool to cool off.

    Having Julian at the party would provide a familiar face even though he might as well as be a stranger too at this point. Given how anti-social Marcy was at school, it was amazing how different she was at work, definitely in her element. (Did the ex-cons have anything to do with it?) Nina had stopped at Just Yogurt on a couple of occasions, during one of Marcy's shifts, just to say hi. Nina wasn't much of a yogurt fan, but Just Yogurt's was delicious. The name was appropriate because yogurt was the only food item that was served, aside from soft drinks, coffee and tea. Back at home, inevitably Marcy was moody and insolent, still stuck in adolescence. Something had to give because Nina felt disrespected in her domain, her daughter acting grown-up when she would so choose. Marcy was in fact at work until 2:00, and she had her own transportation – a used but reliable Ford Focus. Today, Sunday, was when she got off work the earliest.

    Why not be the first one to be given a reading by the psychic? Nina could do so the moment Miss H. arrived, so she could in turn digest everything she was told. (Despite the information being for "entertainment purposes," she was curious to know why Miss H. was considered "accurate.") Nina was the one paying for the psychic's time, so she had as much right to a reading as the party attendees. Being the hostess didn't mean she couldn't partake of her own offerings!

***

Nina spent more time decorating than she'd intended, and she still needed to take a shower and get dressed in case everyone started arriving early, starting with none other than the psychic. Nina removed her jeans while standing in her bedroom, and she was certain she heard rustling in her shoe closet! That would be her ex's (former) walk-in closet, as nowadays she used it just for her footwear, the other walk-in closet for her clothes and accessories.

No scaredy-cat was Nina, so she stuck her head in the closet and looked around, not seeing anyone. Although the chance was remote, someone was possibly in the house because when she was in the backyard decorating, she'd accidentally left the front door unlocked! It was a relatively safe neighborhood, but she wasn't one to take any chances. Nonetheless she obviously just did but refused to obsess over it. She hopped in the shower and didn't give the whole situation another thought.

"I'm coming! I'm coming!" Nina exclaimed as she descended the staircase, dressed in a turquoise, short-sleeved cotton tunic and white pencil-leg jeans and metallic gold, slip-on sandals. Her shoulder-length, silvery blonde hair was still wet from her shower, but she was good to go. For her age she happened to think she looked pretty tremendous.

Anyway, someone was banging the brass lion's head door

Letter to Sarah

knocker. It was either an early party attendee or Miss H. Obviously Nina hoped it was the latter so she could get her pre-party reading. Did Miss H. use tarot cards, read palms or show up with a crystal ball? If the last one was her medium of choice, maybe she toted it in a bowling ball bag!

Nina was still snickering at her silly joke when she opened the front door (she didn't bother looking through the peephole since she was expecting company). Before her on the gray granite stoop was a woman so small she at first looked like a lost little girl. Even though it was a hot day, she was wearing a black nylon scarf over her head, tied under her chin. Her plain black dress was ankle-length but had a V-neck and capped sleeves. The choker she was wearing looked like variously-colored gumballs had been strung together to create it and matched the bracelet on her left wrist. She could have been 18 or 80, it was impossible to tell. One thing was certain: the look in her piercing blue eyes compelled Nina to avert her gaze. She also wanted to slam the door in the woman's face, but she was most likely Miss H., and it was more interesting to have a psychic that made a person uneasy . . . right?

Still giddy, Nina said, "I have to imagine you are none other than —"

"Miss H., that is correct," she said, not waiting for Nina to finish.

Nina wondered if the woman was trying to show her intuition or was just being rude. While pondering that, she introduced herself: "I'm Nina, Marcy's mother. Please come in."

"Thanks, I will. I could also use something to drink."

"I wasn't sure what the party guests would like, so I stocked up on a variety of non-alcoholic beverages." She wanted to point out she was a teetotaler (in addition to being a conscientious parent) but didn't want to appear condescending.

"Never mind," Miss H. said as she followed Nina toward the kitchen, passing the enormous dining room on one side and the even larger living room on the other, both of which were furnished but the latter appeared practically empty because of its size.

Nina couldn't help gauging Miss H.'s reaction to the impressive square footage of the house and in turn gloating a bit. Why not? It had taken a lot of effort to marry, divorce and negotiate a generous settlement from Julian! Finding a decent attorney for the divorce was a lot of work, in and of itself, which helped explain why she was still enjoying her "down time." Nina then witnessed Miss H. pull a shiny silver flask from somewhere in her dress and proceed to swill it! Quickly Nina turned back around and pretended not to have noticed. She realized then she was even more unsettled by Miss H. than she'd thought. It was a good thing Nina had no idea Miss H. stuck her tongue out at her.

Before Nina suggested she be given a reading, she turned on the oven to start baking some finger sandwiches consisting of buttered rye bread with sausage slices and shredded cheddar cheese. There were also some chilled offerings in the refrigerator, for anyone who was "feeling the heat": cucumber and carrot slices topped with Ranch dressing and chopped bacon bits ("real" bacon, not the pre-packaged kind); and cold chicken fingers on a serving tray with four kinds of dipping sauce.

Nina hadn't turned her back on Miss H. for more than a couple seconds and just like that she disappeared! The woman really was rude, wandering off in a house that sure as hell wasn't hers. At first Nina had to stay put, she was so angry. Then she laughed, imagining Miss H. running upstairs to join whoever was hiding in Nina's closet. Of course it was a joke, as it was not something Nina would appreciate were it true. There was no safe for her expensive jewelry, so Miss H. had better not try to use her psychic powers to figure out where it was kept.

From the garage, a car door was slammed shut. Marcy was back from work. She could be the one to look for Miss H.

Letter to Sarah

before changing from her Just Yogurt uniform into something for the party. Nina would take a pass on a reading from Miss H. because she was too disgusted with her. The woman would just be guessing stuff anyway, and who cared what she had to say at this point? Nina could make up something and be just as right.

Nina waited for close to a minute for Marcy to emerge from the garage before walking over to the door leading to it. She was shaking her head in exasperation. Any other than time but today it was unimportant if Marcy lingered in the garage cleaning her car out or whatever she was up to. Nina wanted her to help keep the party organized. It hadn't even started, yet it felt like it was getting out of hand!

Just as Nina finally saw the door knob turn, she felt something slam the back of her head. Immediately she thought perhaps it had to do with the "serious illness" she'd had in eighth grade. She was embarrassed to admit she'd fallen off a picnic table at Hayden Park, hit the back of her head and severely cracked her skull. Even though she had completely recovered, her mother, Jeanne, always feared Nina could have recurring issues, later in life. (Her mother was also a worry-wort.)

Nina stumbled forward, trying not to lose her balance. Then she was hit in the back of her head a second time, and she fell onto the oak plank floor, out cold.

***

"I told you, Dad, Mom drinks like all the time," Marcy told her father when he showed up at her graduation party and he was shown his unconscious ex-wife. "Her habit is so bad she hides it so it looks like she never touches a drop." It was enjoyable telling her father a total lie about her mother because if he was half as smart as everyone acted like he was, he'd figure out the truth, himself!

Mom would be upset if she knew her toasty sandwiches

in the oven got burned. Guests started arriving soon after Dad had carried Mom upstairs to her bed, so no one was paying any attention until there was a burning smell.

The only thing that almost messed up Marcy's plan was when Dad picked up Mom he'd remarked, "Funny, I don't smell any alcohol on her breath."

Fortunately, Miss H. was nearby and said, "Vodka, most likely."

Dad nodded and Miss H. glared at him and stuck out her tongue after he'd turned away. Marcy thought that was extremely disrespectful and almost said something. However, she was honestly afraid of her and wished she hadn't befriended her. This was only the beginning.

Mother Knows Best

"Because I want you to learn the value of money," Linda Betts told her daughter, Marianne, when asked why she needed to get a job for the summer. That sounded preferable to something like, "Because if you have too much free time, you're only going to get into trouble." Marianne was the type who would in turn look for it (trouble) if given half a chance. It wasn't easy raising her basically alone, even though Linda was "happily married." Jacob (Marianne's father) traveled extensively for his career in aeronautics. He was determined a daughter should be raised by her mother and that was that. Since Marianne didn't have a brother it was impossible for "Jacob's Law" to be put to the test.

Long ago Linda stopped lamenting to her mother, Helen, about Jacob's "hands-off approach" in regard to raising Marianne. Time and again Helen would say, "If he's providing well for you and your family, then you have nothing to complain about." She was correct, but Linda had a nagging feeling the real issue was Marianne wasn't turning out right. She had everything she could want yet was bored with life—at seventeen years old! Granted, Oakdale, Indiana wasn't the most exciting place, but downtown Chicago was only fifty minutes away. At Marianne's age Linda and her friends took turns borrowing a vehicle (from a parent) in order to go shopping or just hang out somewhere interesting. Most everyone Linda knew had a part-time job throughout the year, not just for the summer. If it wasn't possible to get a ride to and from work, you walked or rode a bicycle. If it was too far, you got a job that was closer to home.

Marianne did have a couple friends, but one was away for the entire summer, working at a relative's resort in New Jersey and the other one had a job locally. As it was, Marianne's whole world existed inside her phone and nothing much else appeared to matter. However, Linda intended to make her at least appreciate earning a living, even if she didn't yet have to support herself. Although Marianne had but one year left of high school, she refused to discuss the possibility of attending college, even a commuter college. At this rate that talk was never going to take place. Marianne had gotten to the point if she heard any mention about college, she'd cover her ears and loudly say, "Blah, blah, blah," until Linda gave up and turned away!

"I know the value of money, Mom," Marianne told her mother. "I hardly ever ask for any and I don't have that many things. Monica Lorenz has a 'junk room' at her house because she has so much stuff it won't fit in her bedroom. And her bedroom is way, way bigger than mine."

"Who exactly is she? That doesn't sound like someone I ever heard you mention before."

"She's the one who moved here from Dayton after New Year's. Her family bought that three-story house at the corner of Main and East Streets."

"Oh. Obviously you've been to her house. How come you never mentioned her name before?"

After rolling her eyes Marianne replied, "Mom, I have friends besides Karen and Samantha. It just doesn't seem like it because I don't have a reason to talk about them. See? Something like this proves why!"

Linda wished she would have had a son. Even if Jacob reneged on his tenet to raise a boy, maybe at least this kind of conversation could have been avoided. It was apparently inevitable between a mother and a daughter because Linda did it too, when she was Marianne's age. Linda told her, "All I ask is, as I proposed a few minutes before, could you please

Letter to Sarah

find a job for the summer, even if it's delivering newspapers?"

Following another eye roll Marianne stated, "I will, first thing in the morning." Then her phone chimed and she read a text before adding, "Karen just confirmed meeting me on her lunch break. There's a Chinese carry-out place next to the eye doctor's where she works."

"Is Manor View on Broadway the strip mall you're referring to?"

"Yeah."

"There's a gift shop in that mall, called 'Anita's Trinkets,' and a 'Help Wanted' sign was in the window when I happened to pass by the day before yesterday, dropping off a couple of your father's suits at 'Value-U Cleaners' next door. Why don't you see if there's still a position of some sort available?"

"I guess I could," Marianne said but rolled her eyes again after turning away from her mother. She really was a pain. Only after Marianne was finished visiting with Karen and had her fill of shrimp eggrolls would she go in the gift shop and apply for a job. If she waited until tomorrow and the position was finally taken she'd never hear the end of it. She assumed the job being offered was for a cashier, which sounded so boring! Karen worked for Dr. Diehl, answering the phone and making appointments. That seemed slightly more interesting if only because Karen revealed she "played around on the computer" when she didn't have to do work-related stuff. Marianne probably wouldn't have access to a computer, so she'd have to make do with her phone. That was O.K., actually. It would be like getting paid to do what she'd sit around the house doing anyway!

***

Karen and Marianne sat on a concrete bench encircling a maple tree, in front of Red Dragon. Karen had thirty minutes for lunch and had invited her friend because she seemed

Amy Kristoff

especially aimless lately. However, Marianne had recently been told by her mother she had to get a job, and that appeared to have brought her out of her funk, at least temporarily. Karen had in fact wanted to mention there was a 'Help Wanted' sign in the gift shop near the doctor's office where she worked, but she'd feared Marianne wouldn't appreciate it. Karen probably would have told Marianne off, had she reacted belligerently to the news about the job opening. As it was, their mutual friend was Samantha, who was out East for the summer, working at a relative's resort. She always managed to make Marianne seem slightly more interesting. Otherwise Marianne was obsessed with her phone and had a hard time even noticing the world around her. Merely walking the short distance from her car to the front of Red Dragon, she was staring at something on it.

Anyway, Karen was saving for a car, and Marianne already had one: a gray Mitsubishi Lancer. It wasn't new, but it ran great yet Marianne griped about how terrible it was in the snow last winter, the first year she had it. (Her parents bought it for her.) In fact, it was parked in the diagonal space closest to them, the rear of the car facing them. Marianne complained a lot as it was, reminding Karen of her great-grandma Cooper. She was like ninety-six, so that alone vouched for her crankiness.

Marianne mostly wanted to ponder what the job at Anita's Trinkets might entail and was temporarily uninterested in her phone, so Karen pretended to listen while she ate fried rice and texted back and forth with her boyfriend, Duane. Maybe that was Marianne's problem—she needed a date. Karen's brother, Robert, just broke up with his girlfriend, both of whom were nineteen. Karen was going to suggest he go out with someone younger and then bring up Marianne. They were certainly alike in one way: it was impossible to tell what either one was really thinking sometimes. Marianne could be kind of sneaky, while Robert could be outright haughty, no warning whatsoever. Those two might get

Letter to Sarah

each other like nobody's business.

A perfect example of Robert's occasionally hostile attitude: Usually Karen could count on a ride to and from work from her father, as he happened to own a title company a few miles further west on Broadway, the same street Manor View strip mall was on. However, he had an office meeting at five and would be late. Her mother was in Indianapolis for the day, attending a seminar of some kind (she was a loan officer). The point was Karen needed her brother to give her a ride home this one time, yet he acted like it would kill him to pick her up. He was a plumbing apprentice, had his own transportation (a used Jeep Wrangler), and typically was home by four-thirty and sat around the remainder of the day, although sometimes he went out in the evening, "visiting friends." (Karen was certain he sold drugs.) If it hadn't been too far to walk to "Prairie Trail" subdivision, where she lived, Karen would have done so. It occurred to her to ask Marianne if she could pick her up, as she too lived in that subdivision, but it was possible she'd make as big a deal out of the favor as Robert!

Karen never again intended to spend any one-on-one time with Marianne. In the future, when Samantha invited Marianne to tag along with them, Karen wouldn't protest. However, she decided Marianne was a killjoy and didn't appreciate her company. Robert and Marianne really needed to make a go of it.

***

Marianne wished she could say she applied for a job at Anita's Trinkets. She even wished she could say she made a purchase. There was in fact a stolen item from the store, sitting on the passenger seat of her car! It was a stained glass blue jay, which had been in the window, beneath the Help Wanted sign! She would have hocked the suction cup too, but from further inside the store the saleswoman had asked,

Amy Kristoff

"Can I help you?" just as Marianne was stuffing the suncatcher in her beige leather, bucket-style purse. Grabbing the suction cup would have been a dead giveaway. Then again, considering how oblivious the saleswoman was to what Marianne did, it had been tempting to push her luck. In all the excitement, Marianne ended up completely forgetting about applying for a job! As it was, stealing the blue jay was entirely compulsive, as Marianne had never before stolen anything. Actually, she wanted to turn her car around and take the item back but feared the subsequent repercussions. Therefore, she would go home with her stolen loot and vow to never again steal anything. Following the theft she'd considered browsing for a couple minutes but was much too nervous, so she'd told the saleswoman she'd stepped inside the store "by mistake," in response to the question regarding if she needed help. She then explained she'd intended to go in the cleaners. Since Marianne had no real reason to go in there, it was only logical to head straight for her car after leaving the gift shop. Besides, the saleswoman never even showed her face and remained in the back of the store, so she wouldn't notice Marianne failed to go to the cleaners. In fact, a woman with shoulder-length brown hair and wearing blue jeans and a yellow T-shirt just went in there, and Marianne happened to be dressed almost identically! A quick glance and the saleswoman would have thought it was Marianne.

Only once Marianne had reached the street she lived on, Sycamore, did she realize she hadn't thought of an excuse for having failed to at least inquire about the position at Anita's Trinkets. She'd been so razzed after hocking the blue jay, all she'd concentrated on was trying to contain her emotions. Her mother would be really disappointed, but Marianne would simply tell her she forgot, which was the truth! That proved she was honest, overall.

"Prairie Trail" was the cookie-cutter subdivision where Sycamore Street was located. All the houses were two-story,

Letter to Sarah

around twenty-five hundred square feet with three-car garages, typically a two-space door on one side, a single space door on the other. In the case of the Betts family, the single space portion of the garage was relegated to "stuff," which was surprising because her parents were otherwise so fastidious. Since Marianne wasn't allowed to move any of it out of the way nor get rid of it, her car was parked in front of the closed garage door. That way, if either one of her parents needed to back his or her vehicle out, Marianne didn't have to move her car. Granted, Marianne's father was often out of town (or even the country), but Marianne still parked in the same spot no matter what. He in fact happened to be in Houston for a couple days and had driven his Lexus sedan to O'Hare, so she was aware that space was available. However, since she didn't have a garage door remote of her own, she would have had to go inside the garage to open the door with the wall switch.

Marianne unlocked the side door of the garage and found out her mother's blue Volvo sedan was missing, so she wasn't home, either. That gave Marianne a reprieve from having to tell her mother she'd "forgotten" to apply for a job at Anita's Trinkets.

Just as Marianne was about to go in the house, she heard a vehicle pull in the driveway and the engine was turned off. She became extremely nervous but had the wherewithal to use "the stuff" to her advantage by sticking the blue jay inside a large, black plastic tote that was filled with old tax returns, which seemed like a dumb thing to leave in the garage. She prepared to go outside and find out who had followed her home, assuming someone had witnessed her stealing the suncatcher, after all. This part of the situation could have been avoided if her stupid parents had cleared a space for her car and given her a remote control for the door!

Marianne literally about s—t when her mother appeared in the side garage doorway, looking extremely angry. In fact

Amy Kristoff

Marianne noticed her expression first and then processed the realization her mother was wearing the same outfit as whoever Marianne just witnessed entering the cleaners.

"You ready?" Marianne's mother finally asked her.

"Where are—"

"To take the stained glass blue jay back to 'Anita's Trinkets.'"

Her mother looked incensed enough to slap her, and Marianne felt like she deserved it. Instead her mother watched while Marianne retrieved the blue jay from the tote. Then she said, "I told the proprietor about what you did and that you were supposed to have applied for the job she has available . . . or at least ask about it. Turns out she is trying to offer online ordering and was hoping a young adult applied for the position because he or she would know more about computers than her. That young adult would have to be very trustworthy, something you clearly aren't."

Marianne took her sweet time getting in her mother's Volvo but not because she was staring at her phone. She'd left it on top of the tote. She wished she'd noticed this car in the parking lot, as well as what her mother was wearing earlier.

About the Author

Amy has written several novels and short story collections, including a trio of books with off-beat dog themes. She lives on a horse farm in Indiana. AmyKristoff.com.

Printed in the USA
CPSIA information can be obtained
at www.ICGtesting.com
JSHW021027180924
69820JS00002B/13